# THERE AND NEVER, EVER BACK AGAIN

---

## A DARK LORD'S JOURNAL

### JEFFREY MACH

PUBLISHED BY FASTPENCIL PUBLISHING

There And NEVER, EVER BACK AGAIN

First Edition

Print edition ISBN: 9781499905809

http://www.fastpencil.com

Printed in the United States of America

# TABLE OF CONTENTS

# Dedication and Prologue

*To the Moon, and to all the Orcs in the world.*

### Acknowledgments:

This book owes a great debt to its amazing Beta Readers, especially **Harley Kallisti**. It also would not have been possible without the help and support of **The Critter**, **The Family**, **Mr. David Isecke**, **P'tah**, and, of course—as always—**Evil Expo**, and the ever-inspiring **#TeamVillain**.

### Metaphysics:

The world is made of Names, and "names". Sometimes it's impossible for a human to know which one is being invoked. So I've tried to capitalize where appropriate, and lowercase when not; but when one is guessing at the fabric of Reality and/or reality, one ought to expect to err sometimes. If that bothers you, just assume that every time I say "humans" instead of "Humans", or "Dark" instead of "dark", it's based on a complex and ornate linguistic structure which has been fully developed in my mind. That might even be true.

### Benediction:

"Such horrible things live under the bed
(Keep handy the funeral wreath)
But I was the one who crept under the bed
And ate the Monster beneath."

# INTRODUCTION

There is a white wizard, cloaked in spellcraft and guile and a truly astonishing sense of self-righteousness, and *he simply will not stop slaughtering The Chosen One until he kills me.*

He must be quite a sight to the unknowing. He has an actual white horse (I genuinely suspect he painted the poor beast) – and there he is, riding ramrod-straight into some tiny village or hamlet which had previously known him primarily for his card tricks. Now he looks neither left nor right (which is problematic for oncoming traffic, and many a vegetable cart is overturned in the wake of his utter disregard for basic vehicular courtesy) – but presses steadily forward until he reaches a certain hut.

Then, eyes blazing like a carelessly-started forest fire, he raps imperiously on the door with his sorcerous stave. He informs the bewildered parents that he must see their offspring (he seems to have a habit of picking only children, for reasons about which I prefer not to speculate at this time.) He gazes at the aforementioned moppet with a disturbing thousand-yard stare, and then suddenly proclaims that this is the Child of Prophecy, the Chosen One, the mortal destined to bring down the Dark Lord.

The parents seldom complain. The cause is so terribly just, the kids do eat a lot, and besides, you know what they say about wizards—"Never piss off a crazy person with a magical boom stick."

So they pack the sprog off, with a few tears and a brave smile, and perhaps some pride and hope.

They never see the kid again.

Look, let's be honest. Even a *tiny* patrol of Orcs is more than a match for your average pre-adolescent, regardless of whether or not you've got a couple of underemployed companions along for the ride. Maybe that Wizard could do something, but he's never around. There's always some nebulous task he must accomplish, some vital but secret mission. He promises he'll meet up with them later.

But he won't. He's off weaponizing some other urchin. Because he figures that, if he keeps throwing them at me, one of them will get through.

There's a vanishingly small survival rate among Chosen Ones.

*Hey, is that a knock at your door?*

# PART I:

THERE IS NOTHING TO FEAR EXCEPT THE MANIAC WHO
KEEPS TELLING YOU THERE'S NOTHING TO FEAR

# How To Construct A Chosen One

It is essential, first off, that your Chosen One be pure of heart, or, to put it more directly, naive as hell.

After all, there's this prophecy and/or the word of some hypothetical authority figure telling her to go off, fight impossible odds and (if one is at all realistic about this) probably die.

It takes more than idealism or a sense of duty to make a person do something like that. It also takes someone who is willing to believe in a mission both preposterous *and* life-threatening. It takes someone easily led—or misled—by rather dubious sources.

From watching the Wizard's methods, I'll note that it tends to help if you find subject who is unreasonably optimistic about the potential for good in the world. Or someone *terribly* credulous.

True, longterm, you'll have trouble with the easily led; presumably, at some point, the kid will have to show enough self-direction to get past puzzles, or mazes, or simply challenges which test one's mettle to the breaking point. If you ain't got the mettle, then you break--ka-SNAP!

Then again, there are a *lot* of potential candidates for Chosen One. And anyone who can do enough math to do magic knows your essential brute force algorithm: Just keep throwing resources at the problem, and eventually, you'll exhaust the possibilities and find an answer.

So if you lose one, or two, or ten Chosen Ones, sure, a few rumours might circulate back. And people might begin being reluctant to join you. But that's okay. You have Good on your side, and that means you get to keep on Choosing.

His method's quite simple, really. Just walk up to a house and pick somebody. Who's going to question the living embodiment of Benevolence and All Things Bright and Sunlit?

Only Bad people do that. And you don't want to be a bad person...*right*?

Nor do you want your friends, neighbors, associates, rulers, and assorted strangers to hear you've been branded as "Not Good" by an authority on Good. You don't want *that*, do you? After all, all gotta do is go along. It's a noble cause. Why wouldn't you help a noble cause?

You're not *for* the Dark Lord, are you?

You're not *on the side of the Dark Lord, are you*?

And you're surely not *the Dark Lord in disguise*, right? Because if you were, we'd have to take appropriate action. Your house *is* a bit gloomy, and didn't a neighbor hear you mention, some time back, by the village well, that you thought life under a Dark Lord might be an improvement?

That's not what you said? It sounded like that. That's how your neighbor remembers it. In fact, now that your neighbor has brought it up, it appears that *several* of your neighbors were at the well. They *all* remember hearing you say that, and lots more; seems like everybody's got a story. The well was crowded that day. They're all in the pub now, buying each other drinks. It's amazing how vivid their memories are. Hey, the bartender just remembered being there, too!

They're all *such* good people. Pretty brave of them to stand up and speak in the face of all the Dark Powers you might have.

But you're probably not past redemption. Not yet.

So—about your love of the Dark Lord. You'd like to fix that, wouldn't you? All we need is the kid...and don't worry. The kid will be just fine.

We'll learn it *real* good.

(Time passes. People die.)

But that stuff doesn't happen too often. Doesn't have to. There are lots of targets, and it's easy to pick a ripe one. Hell, you need look no further than the average family life in this realm. You might ask: What kind of parents would permit an offspring to head off blithely towards likely doom?

Bad parents, for one. Neglectful, abusive, or just plain uncaring people are a *great* start. If your Chosen One has some of these, she'll go *running* towards an alternative, especially if you throw in some kind of father figure, some kindly, benevolent spellcasting dispenser of life-affirming quotes and life-destroying missions.

Give someone a sufficiently broken domestic upbringing, and you've got lots of options for eager urchins.

Why are so many Chosen Ones unpopular in their societies and neighborhoods? It's because, in its secret mechanisms, the Universe actually works in such a way that kids who are bullied and put-upon turn out to have the most golden destinies imaginable.

Nah, I'm just messing with you; that's *ridiculous*, and no sensible being would believe that for a moment. The real reason the White Wizard loves to pick students who aren't accepted by those around them? Well, for starters, if you want to insure yourself some prime, dedicated-to-the-death, unquestioning, I-will-do-the-craziest-damn-things-for-reasons-that-don't-make-sense-but-which-you-say-are-essential Chosen meat, start off with someone who's disdained, ill-treated, or even actively attacked for who and what they are. Tell them there's *a whole other world*, one where they're special. Tell them it's their *destiny*. Tell them it's what they *deserve*.

O Gods, we give thanks unto thee for the bounty with which thou hast provided us. And also the Hobbit-weed.

Remember, you're not *lying*, exactly. You're just leaving out a few key details, like, "Right now, you're special because you've got a pulse and you're willing to come along. But survive more than two weeks, and you'll be something *quite* unusual: a statistical anomaly".

Other factors? There are a few. Absent parents are good. Pro tip: Orphans. They're often scared, vulnerable, and lonely. They're ready for brainwashing—oh, sorry, I forget. When the heroes do it, it's called "training".

And, of course, there are also just plain *foolish* parents. Maybe they're royalty who confuse primogeniture with destiny. Maybe they'll just believe anyone who tells them that they represent Good and it's time to defeat Evil. Oversimplified Manichaeism is terribly persuasive; it's simply so much more *fun* to believe that you must be Right, and someone else must be Wrong, *deeply, cosmically wrong*. There's not a lot in this world as motivational as a firm belief in an unbending universal morality which just *happens* to place you on the side of the angels.

Actually, regardless of lineage, your Chosen One is likely to need that kind of simplistic worldview to be really receptive to your Wise And Kindly Wizard.

And that's where traditional narratives fail.

The White Wizard would have you believe that the fall of the Dark Lord is destiny. But if he *really* felt that way, he wouldn't look so damn worried all the time.

Dark Lords **shatter** destiny; it's what we do. The rise of darkness is *not* inevitable (and neither is the rise of light). We may enjoy our metaphors of night and day, but those are really just natural phenomena, literally the product of objects and forces larger than the planet upon which we stand, and not the mystical embodiments of Good and Bad We're not inherently dwellers in illumination or shadow; we're sentients, which means we choose.

And not only am I not part of anyone's damn destiny, nobody predicted my rise—not even me, really. I didn't know this was where I'd end up, and if you try to tell me that the hurt, the pain, the personal choices, and the perseverance were all just part of someone else's plan, I'll laugh at you until I can barely breathe.

When I started out, all I knew was that I was *not* going to stay where I'd been. I was going to change. I was going to make my part of the world into something that I wanted—not wait, hope, or beg for the world to start to want me.

That's why the Wizard looks so grim; it's why so many have failed; it's why this will never be a simple task. Because I didn't get to this place from some cakewalk down a preordained path which said, "And today will be born one of great power"; I had to *find* the damn power, harness it, and not (*yet*) die in the process.

I have tremendous strength, but it's not really in the magic, or the realm I've built around me, the tools or the technology. It's the result of what it took for me to get here, and what I have shaped myself into becoming. I am a product of the flames which burnt me; the anvil which forged me; and the will that made me grow formidable instead of breaking.

All these things mean that "Destiny" can go climb a rope. To defeat a Dark Lord, you can't just have a pretty astrological chart. You must have exceptional puissance. And an unexamined world-view is a *deep and abiding weakness*. It's an underdevelopment of critical thinking skills. It lets you skate right past moral ambiguity, which is helpful until suddenly becomes a detriment. The person who has never wrestled with "why" has missed a crucial battle. It Is possible that, without having endured and survived that fight, you are not prepared to handle the bitter path that leads to my door.

Poor Chosen One.

The person who has never considered "non servium" may have a fatal weakness in the legs. Train yourself to kneel instead of think, and you will *not* enjoy an opponent who knows how to stand.

# On Some Fundamentals of Dark Magic

At this moment, the Chosen One is being inculcated with the idea that I do Dark Magic, and thus I am most thoroughly evil. I'm pretty certain the White Wizard has a fairly expansive knowledge of the subject, and I'm not exactly sure where he gets all this stuff about the use of virgins for altars, or strange rites of the forest involving a great deal of wine and very little clothing.

I really think the White Wizard needs to get out more.

(Either that, or he's confusing me with Dionysus. I suspect the White Wizard really believes that, somewhere along the paths of learning, there were all manner of secret and terrible rituals to which he was not invited. I mean, totally, he missed out on a kegger or two, but honestly, you should have heard that guy go on when he had a few drinks in him; *unbearable*. For a being of awe and wonder, that son of a crossbow sure can ramble on.)

But speaking of rambling. I digress. So, is Dark Magic evil?

No. Think about it: How would that even work?

Or to ask a more relevant question, *what would it take for magic to be evil?*

This might seem simple on the face of it, but it ain't. For starters, morality's not static. In one age, we fight and die for the divinity of the monarchy; to contest that is to go against all the decency in the world. In the next era, we overthrow the monarchy, and perhaps consider the entire institution to be utterly and completely wicked. After *that*, perhaps we believe that each individual should be treated based on merit. And *then* we fight over what's meritorious and what's suddenly worthless...

In other words, the incantation which slays a king is monstrous in one epoch, heroic in another, pointless in a third. How would the *magic* know which is which?

I'll grant that magic is an unpredictable, semi-sentient, capricious force (telling magic "Do as you will!" is much the same as telling a Grand Vizier "Oh, nobody's counted the treasury in years, and we lost the key, too, but hey, we're sure all those rubies the size of plums and those emeralds the size of fists are just *fine*.") Noting that Magic has something like intelligence, and therefore *might* be capable of possessing moral qualities, we still run afoul of many rocky questions. Can "light" and "dark" be determined by your motivations? In other words, does magic read your intentions?

My dear sweet collection of glands and stimulus responses, you may not know your *own* heart completely, and the same goes for your soul. Do you expect sorcery to both do your bidding *and* diagnose your innermost desires? Magick is untapped power stolen from the laws of physics when the Universe wasn't looking; it's not your therapist.

Then, after intention—what about consequence? If magic is somehow inherently good or bad, then it surely needs to understand not only *why* you desire to do something, but what the effects will be. Context matters. If you *intend* to save a person who is drowning, and *instead* sink a fully-crewed ship, is that white magic or black?

Ponder how much processing power we would need in order for magic to be "evil" by *any* definition at all. It's *significantly* more than what's requisite for even fairly powerful spells. Killing a human being, for example, doesn't actually take all that much sorcerous work; a slight surge of electricity into a heart, the coincidence of a misdriven vehicle, the errant entrance of bacteria into a morsel of food; the brief moment of lethargy which makes you stay in the bed of someone else's marital partner for just a minute longer than is prudent.

(The difference between "fate", "bad luck", and "a magical action determined to achieve your death" can be measured in inches, much like the arrow that misses you by just a little bit, versus the one which merrily opens your femoral artery.)

These are minor alterations of reality; fairly simple, compared to the giant work of metaphysics involved in making a work of magic "evil".

Like many things, if you seek simple answers to complex things (in other words: if you're going to be too lazy to really consider the problem), you start running into difficulties *immediately*. Take a common thought—"Magic which kills a human being is Dark Magic". Is it, though? If "killing" was a mark of evil, who'd suddenly be a villain? Not just soldiers in wars, but also doctors who try and fail (or don't try hard enough); bad carriage drivers; the makers of that one deep-fried pork-stuffed turkey leg that they do over at the Pig and Poke tavern on Grease Street...

No. The only reason we're able to do anything other than the most basic enchantment is because all these considerations come from the human side—the interpretation, the names we give to certain spellwork, the way others tell the story later. It isn't inherent to the *spells*. Classifying magic poorly is an error made by those who want to pin it down and twist it into a shape which pleases them. It ain't the the fault of the living paranormal power which pervades the Multiverse.

Here's the way this really plays out:

If it's outside of what is accepted, if it argues with the Lore, if it seeks to do that which is said to be impossible, then suddenly, according to the White Wizards and their ilk, it can't be "light". Apparently, if it's not something we've already seen and done, if it's not something that has a natural home under the Sun, then it is to be feared.

To the Hells with that. Dark Magic is merely spellcraft which is found in the cracks, the holes, the hidden "dark places" where ordinary magic leaves off. Dark Magic begins when the assembled Lore says, "This, you cannot do", and you reply,

"Why not?"

It's not simply about defiance, of course. I might not agree with every grimoire, but I've sought and found and read every single strangely-bound collection of oddly-dancing words I could possibly find. (That's part of why I'm writing this; always try to leave the ladder with more rungs than when you found it.) And all the runework and the study and the alchemy and the conjurings and the battles of wits with the speaking dead, they're essential, as well, if you would pursue a left-hand path. You can't gain sorcerous dominion without the work and the risk.

This is the heart of a Dark Lord. This is why societies—rightfully, mind you—push us out. Society *needs* those who are abhorrently different; from us come science, medicine, homicide, religion, cultural improvement and cultural disruption. Society needs us, but it often doesn't want us.

We become their leaders, their witch-doctors, their eccentrics—or their ostracized.

*That* is what makes our magick dark. We question the world. We question our realities. We seek out *change* when *sameness* is safety and comfort. We are makers and shatterers. We are phoenixes; both incineration, and new birth. We're not the only ones who do that. But we're the ones who fit in least. And when you don't put in the effort to fit in, you signal that you are some kind of threat to the culture. Even if you might be a *positive* threat, you still activate societal antibodies.

So all dark magic starts with stepping outside of unseen barriers, not of magic, but of tradition and taboo. They fear you, so they name you after the things which terrify them--the primordial night, the unseen, the unknown.

Is there such a thing as Dark Magic?

If there isn't, *make some.*

# MAKING A MONSTROUS ARMY

I have never met an Orc with decent self-esteem.

Contrary to popular belief, Orcs are not ugly. They're frequently asymmetrical, which can be jarring to other sentients, since normal humanoid bilateral symmetry tends to see deviation from regularity as deformity. (Yet we claim not to fear malformed humans; is that true?)

Oh, the cave-dwellers have tusks, sure. That's a reason to dislike their faces. Then again, we fear the canines of the Orc...but we enjoy those of the dog. Why is that?

It's because dogs are domesticated, unthreatening. If they were sentient, we might call them slaves.

Orcs refuse to be slaves to Man. And Man can't handle it.

The Orcs and I have a long understanding. Because I provide them with a target-rich environment? Sure, that's a bit of it. But I actually offer something better and far more meaningful. I accept them.

For humans believe that Man and Orc cannot coexist. Humans say that the Orcs are vicious predators who would see everyone else dead or in servitude.

And of course, humans wouldn't lie, would they?

They never do that.

They surely asked the Orcs before labelling them as enemies.

Because that's consistent with human history, is it not?

Humans have pretty much never recorded an encounter with Orcs that ended in peace.

That's *got* to be the Orcs' fault.

Humans believe that Orcs need extermination. Personally, I believe they need therapy.

I don't make monsters.

Definitions make monsters.

You make definitions.

Do you know why you fear the things that go bump in the dark?

*Because you're the ones who drove them into the dark to begin with.*

# On How To Win Friends and Enemies, And Then Kill Them Both

Since this appears to be the moment at which The Chosen One is gathering her band of stout-hearted, deathwish-possessing colleagues, it might be a good time to talk about alliances.

(How they flock to her now, guided by the reputation of the sage at her side. It's very dramatic that they're all risking death, of course. On the other hand, in your ordinary medieval-era culture, the average lifespan is about 40. There's a reason Beowulf wasn't particularly planning on a long retirement.)

Still, who would possibly dare to step forward in front of a multitude and promise that they'll put their lives on the line to uphold ultimate good? Anyone who likes parades, getting laid, and having drinks bought for them in taverns, that's who.

It would be cynical to say that the White Wizard gathers allies because he wants to be surrounded by admirers. It would also leave out the fact that he likes to be surrounded by an abundance of meat shields in case something goes wrong.

In contrast to the Wizard's widespread appeal, it's sometimes said that Dark Lords care and are cared about by none but themselves. That is primarily a discussion for later, but it does open a few pestiferous questions that the forces of Light tend to leave out of their calculations on a distressingly regular basis. Starting with:

*How in the Eleven Hells would that even work?*

Seriously, who would ally with someone whose goodwill is based entirely on convenience? Why fight, other than very temporarily, beside someone who will supposedly turn on you as soon as their own objectives are achieved? If Dark Lords won't remain true to their words, if they're consistently treacherous, how would they ever raise up armies?

Either one would need a steady stream of lies, or a convenient superabundance of overly-foolish allies. In either case, bear in mind that gullible comrades are a weak spot; after all, if *you* can deceive them consistently, that does not speak well of their ability to see through the ruses and feints of your enemies. Anyone who'll fall for "Oh, your friend who was asking inconvenient questions? Managed to slip and land on his own ten-foot halberd. Very sad" – yeah, anyone who'll believe that more than, say, zero times is going to be utterly at a loss the next time an enemy army pretends to charge them, and flanks around in a pincer motion instead.

But hey! Heroic deaths are exciting, right?

So okay. Assume some of your allies are just idiots. That can't be the whole truth, so the rest must be taken in by the aforementioned constant stream of falsehoods–

Yes, that's one way to do it. But it presupposes the idea that The Dark Lord is one miserable son of a bitch. Because this would bring us to another logical question: Why amass tremendous power only to live a lie?

Theorize that Dark Lords are, as claimed, simply evil beings of deception with no motivation to do anything other than act in their own benefit. Even were this the case, the whole problem of living a lie is that you become known for what you are *not*, instead of what you *are*.

That's *not* beneficial to you. It's pretty pointless to fight your way towards power, only to lose the identity which made the fight worthwhile.

Why become Dark Lord simply to enact the fantasies of others? Why struggle through all that pain and difficulty only to be a character actor?

And how do you plan to get anywhere if you don't have a consistent model of reality which interacts well with the outside world? Propaganda hits the emotions just fine, but doesn't translate well into accomplishment. For example, a few Chosen Ones back, the White Wizard told one of his protégés, "Fear not the night, for you carry within you the light of truth."

Kid was eaten that same night by a boggart. If there was any light inside that youngster, all it did was serve as seasoning.

The White Wizard has promised an end to the reign of Darkness, by which I believe he means some anthropomorphic personification of evil.

It doesn't make much logical sense, but it sure sounds exciting.

I've promised my allies the Sun.

We'll see who lied, later.

# I DIDN'T CHOOSE THE EXILED-AT-SPEARPOINT LIFE; THE EXILED-AT-SPEARPOINT LIFE CHOSE ME

Those who begin to summon demons, on seeing something they can't handle coming through the Gate, sometimes abjure: "Come forth, but not in that form!" And by this they mean that they want access to the power, but not the corresponding pain and madness which lap at its fringes.

Sometimes they get what they want. Usually, they get what they deserve.

When I am hard-pressed, I sometimes ask myself: did I ascend a blood-etched throne simply to be the incarnation of someone else's imaginings?

The answer is *never*, *never*, and *never*, and thus reminded, I redouble my efforts and go on.

The people are, as it has been said, a great beast—and no simple, civilized beast like a werewolf or a momrath, but a huge, angry, amorphous mass, all too ready to set fire to anything they don't understand. Individual humans may be wise; large groups of humans have the intellect of rocks, if rocks had the capacity for spite, petty jealousy, and a desire to be entertained by the misfortunes of poorly-dressed celebrities.

They will steal your sense of self, because they'll repeat what they think you are until the murmurs of it echo through the hallways of your home and the alleys of your mind. And to a Dark Lord, the steel bar inside you, that thing you've relied on since the beginning, honed and strengthened, *that sense of self*, is more valuable than the throne. Because with it, if you had to, you could win another throne; without it, you will lose this one.

That's part of why they want to take it away from you. They may not understand on a conscious level, but they recognize you have some quality, something inside, which will not let itself be moved against your will; that it's not inborn, but the product of your own sweat and shaping. They *fear* that thing. And rightly, perhaps; one could do truly horrific things if one is able to choose in favor of her inner mind, instead of the desires of others. Nevermind that one could also thusly make wonders.

They hate being unable to control you; they feel like, when the chips are down, you might decide to act in your own interests instead of theirs.

I will let you in on a little secret: the reason they fear the worst of you is because it is *what they have in their own hearts.*

Most of them do not have the ability to defy a group or a conventional idea on their own. But they know that, if they *could* defy the needs of the group without being stopped, they would steal what they could for themselves, and they assume all others must be the same way. Has the team a cache of gold that none are supposed to touch? They'd take it *if they thought they wouldn't get caught.* They see morality as constant outside pressure: *We force each other to be good, because otherwise, we'd all do evil.*

They don't quite visualize it that way in their heads, of course. They view it in the traditional way: "If we thought we could do so, we'd take the gold...but we'd spend most of it on widows and orphans, of course, where it belongs. But if the Dark One had the gold, she would use it on destruction and folly!"

(I'll freely admit: when I have gold, *folly* is a priority. Give me airships and luftbaloons! Give me rock faces carved into Orcish puns! Give me the ridiculous, because it's a gateway to the sublime. Besides, seriously, have you considered what would happen if you lived for centuries and never laughed? Your expression would probably calcify and you'd have permanent lemonface.

But *destruction?* True, Dark Lords raze things to the ground; we also raise things up. If you're entirely sure that it's the Dark Lords who do all the destroying, and none of the making, I'd like to invite *you* to try to build a realm sometime. If you haven't done what we've done, you may not have a lot of ground from which to criticize.)

All this is part of why some cling so hard to "Good", as if every-thing in the universe had, inscribed somewhere upon its atoms, a little sign that said "**here is good**" or "**here is evil**". They absolute-ly need to believe in Good, and they *need* to believe they're on its side. Because with doubt comes the possibility of being wrong, and once you think there's a chance you could be wrong, you have to deal with that annoying, tricksy little problem: "*What if I'm not doing the right thing?*"

Takes a lot of energy to tackle that one, energy which could much more pleasurably be expended hanging about the pub, talk-ing about your own personal excellence.

And so they seek to be Good, and to be around Good. And they can't see me as having any of its qualities; that would make me a little like them, and they're *terrified* that we might have anything in common. I need to be a beast, and the *only* beast, because only *then* is it appropriate to hunt me without limits.

Good has friends and allies. What does evil have? Presumably a consortium of power-hungry fiends, united either by fear of me, or by deception. Or both, one suppose. Surely evil never has equals. Never has colleagues. Never has those who are joined in bonds of camaraderie; surely something in your spiritual makeup rejects kinship with others, once your soul is tainted.

Good theory, right?

Only if one were really that toxic to others, answer me this:

*Why would you want a world where you can only have friends you will use, but never truly join?*

The obvious answer is that you can use them to secure power, and that's true–up to a point. Yes, power is its own reward. But likewise, some methods of obtaining power are their own punish-ment.

Being without empathy, whether it's inherent or learned, is a weakness. Being unable to share the feelings of those around you would just cut you off from the world, and the less you are asso-ciated with the realm you walk, the less effectively you can make your mark on it.

You may not prefer frequent human contact, be it from intro-version or misanthropy, but if we weren't meant to commune with others, we wouldn't have either language centers in our brains, or taverns. The same beer oughtn't taste better when consumed in the right company...but it *does*. Because human minds are peculiar things.

Oh, there are lots of reasons why you'd *want* cease being human—stop being a tiny, angry, frightened, vicious thing, vulnerable to the contagion of any neighbor with a strong view and some shiny farm implements. You might want to become a God; you might simply want to become Not What You Are.

It's tempting, but again, think longterm. Gods forget the ways and lives of mortals. This doesn't just make for bad rulership. It makes for a bad sense of what humans can do. There's enough force and might trapped inside a bitsy, mortal, hominid body to create—well, to create someone like a Dark Lord, for one thing. Ascend away from that, and you *disconnect*. Mortals are ape and angel, both ephemeral and divine. Life has meaning because it ends; life has purpose, because its potential cannot be named or numbered, only built.

That's a lot of power to give up, in exchange for what is, in effect, a ton of force without an instruction manual. The more you get a reputation for shouting, "I AM A GOD; BOTHER ME NEVER AGAIN, MAYFLIES!" when you're annoyed, the less you're going to win loyalty from anyone else. And the less you'll understand it when the "mayflies" become a hive and then a swarm, *and then they come for you.*

Because you must remember this: If there is ONE thing at which mortals excel, it is at killing their gods. Ask any of the legion of forgotten pantheons who formerly ruled parts of the world. Or read their holy books—if you can find them; if they haven't been destroyed, or rewritten with new names to suit the convenience of the humans who made them.

Without connection, you become a lens which is clear only in one direction, and you project onto others that which you see in your own, badly expurgated self.

That is the misery of the White Wizard, and possibly why he spends quite so much time indulging in Hobbit-weed. He's essentially alone by choice. Since he's laid claim to Good, then he must be friends with those around him; but you can't have friends when all of your allies are expendable. He claims to see, and serve, a bigger picture, and that picture is conveniently large enough to take in the scope of everything around him, yet too narrow to care about the mortality of those who have given him their trust.

I can assure you that when the Council of White Wizards gathers, they speak entirely of the pain of dealing with mortals, of their unbearable stupidity, of how they do not understand the safety and comfort into which they were born. More than one White Wizard believes they ought to simply let all the mortals kill each other or die. They can't see themselves as ever having been mortals; now that they've attained power which separates them from others, they believe those others to have always been sleepers, content to have the world pass them by, uncaring about the harm they wreak.

I know. I was one of them once.

They assuredly believe that I am evil. But I'm also a threat to the image they show to outsiders. For what is a wizard without glamour?

I'm not without my own flaws; hardly. But those who judged me without seeking to understand, those who thought they could find morality through popularity, those who would simplify me into just being on the wrong side of some imagined line between good and evil – no, I don't miss them. But some left my side for reasons towards which I'm more sympathetic. There are too many creatures who might otherwise have been be friends...and are not, because of the very real fear that their people will shun them, and they will end up starved for community. Like me.

Or–if they persist in showing sympathy to the pure Evil I'm told I represent (how does one achieve such a thing? Is it better or worse than "impure evil"?)–they, too, could be cast out.

Humans love the image of the lone wolf, but like the wolf, they are pack animals. That does not mean they aren't individuals. It means that they are guided by subtle motions, by scents, by the cues of feeling and sense in those around them. It is not that none will walk away from the pack; it's that it isn't done lightly. Not every group will let you return.

And exile is an acrid vintage indeed.

(Though I persist in believing this is an error on the part of the Banishers part. If, as a culture, you thrust people out, you run the risk of those same people realizing they like it *better* on the outside.)

# DIARY OF THE CHOSEN ONE: THRILLING ADVENTURES BEGIN

This sucks.

It would take an idiot to be taken in by Master Wizard. An idiot, or someone who really wants to believe.

And I'm sure he thinks I want to believe. Who doesn't, right? Good versus evil, fighting on the side of all things Bright and Shining. What could be more seductive?

I think my dear friend and surrogate (thanks to him) father-figure, the Wizard, is pretty certain that nobody would disagree with him. Like, ever. On anything.

I think that's part of why I started to doubt him—you'd figure this would be the epicenter of his life, when frankly, I think he's kind of bored, and it shows.

I think he's done this before.

I think he's done this a **lot**.

There is a literal, physical blot of darkness over some of the land, floating back and forth, letting light through intermittently. What, exactly, is that supposed to prove? Some plants wither, but some plants thrive (we've passed enough belladonna to hallucinate an entire army of Elves). The Dark Lord doesn't seem interested in purging the surface, just changing it so it's inhospitable to humans.

To be honest, that doesn't seem wholly illogical, since humans have clearly sought to make it inhospitable to the Dark Lord.

And it's my job to go out, avoid being killed, and kill in return. I hope you'll excuse me if I manage to withhold my enthusiasm.

So only **I** can do this? The stars somehow aligned for **me**? All my past misfortunes were merely preparation for where I am today?

Please allow me to note that my past misfortunes never actually required me to literally risk losing my life in order to murder someone I haven't met.

You'll pardon me, I hope, if I'm not precisely excited.

In the end, I'll do what must be done, because that's what matters. Everyone tells me so; who am I to think they're wrong?

I can't let everyone down. And I won't.

It's my life to give up. And I think I would do so willingly. Maybe not for the good of Humanity—I'm not sure humanity is all that good—but because they're my kind.

I mean, I was born human. They were born human. We're in this together. That's more than enough to die for, isn't it?

# You're Probably Doing Something Right If They're Trying To Kill You

The Chosen One has started to encounter proof of evil: Dark things have begun to attack her.

That's certainty, right? The things that come for her are shadowy in appearance and bring to mind Jungian conceptions of demons and monsters; they *must* be evil. The White Wizard was quite poetic about it:

*"Out of the shadows they come; and unless we drive them away, they will infest everything, until there is only shadow."*

Nevermind that the purpose of *any* conspicuous military look is to inspire respect and terror. If an army isn't trying to fade into undetection, then it wants to inspire panic in its enemies. No fighting force of Man or Elf is any different.

(And has anyone mentioned to this fool that shadows are a *contrast*? If everything was darkness, shadows would die. Like all things, they need light.)

Perhaps I ought to cloak my minions in wreathes of glittering light. (It's preposterous to assume that I have the magic to rule a domain, but can't make sparkling, shiny things—as if the physics of refraction relied on some moral code.)

But really, their obfuscated presence is true to their natures. They are what they seem to be: beings of shadow. I'll freely admit that is their nature; the question is, do you understand what that means?

*These are beings who've been pushed out of daylight, and so made the umbra their own.* Let them appear as they have become. Permit them to embrace the dark and be proud, and if some fail to appreciate it what they're seeing, the fault is not with the embracer, but the witness.

There's no end to the physical, metaphorical, psychological, or biological importance of sunlight. Pretty flowers wither without it because they need to convert its rays to energy. Crops die. Animals become sluggish and, eventually, starve. Hell, for most of human history, human activity has slowed or ceased in any place lacking sufficient technology or magic to emulate daytime. It takes centuries of research and work to find tools which let you treat the night like the day.

Humans get that; and yet they don't seem to understand what happens *when they push others out of the light.*

The beasts in the back of your cave, your living space at the dawn of time, the ones still in your head? They are not evil. Just hungry, and better adapted for night vision than you. But they terrify you, perhaps they attack you or kill you in your dreams, and the adrenaline drives you out of the cavern, and the terror makes you gasp, and those physical reactions, later reviewed by your mind, solidify and rationalize: *that which hunted me* was not simply seeking food. It was somehow inherently *wrong.*

Because that's what the mind does. It takes tangles of chemical reaction in the brain, and resolves them into what it sees as answers. Thinking beings seem to have great difficulty in recognizing how often that "thinking" part isn't the primary motivator in their actions—or how hard you need to work in order to begin to change that simple truth.

(*Criticism* is, for some, a human pleasure; *critical thinking* is, for most, at best a burdensome chore.)

Humans don't care what happens when they drive you away from the bright places. Or perhaps they really don't consider it. This seems unbelievably shortsighted; but most beings with enough language to have words for the future manage, somehow, to have a surprising proclivity for disregarding said future. It's peculiar. It might be a coping mechanism, although poor planning doesn't seem to me like it a positive survival trait.

And so we drive things into the murk, and then we wonder why the gloom holds terrors for us. This is part of why incessant night billows out from my stronghold. Because the stuff of night is *potent.* Even a hint of its essence has a profound effect. It frightens; it awes; and it brings humans the discomfort of knowing a little more what life is like for those canceled and cast out. They seem to believe that I'll do this forever; I won't. I have no intention of ruling dust. But I'll do it long enough to etch a reminder into human skulls: This is the back of the cave, and you are not too pure to feel its chilling, alienating, claustrophobic unease.

It's still fascinating, even after all of these years, to see how humans believe that surrounding themselves with physical light means, not simply safety, but moral righteousness. It's symptomatic of a larger problem: Evil enthralls us, but Good is what we claim to expect of each other. What could be better than to cloak yourself in Good, giving yourself the assurance that it means there can be no evil underneath?

There is a sensual pleasure in righteousness. This is part of the ugly truth of the Puritan.

Humans process positive sensations in a number of fascinating ways. The sensory apparatus sends data, the mind takes hold of it and parses it, and the consciousness develops response. It's not always a logical, rational, or wise response. Happy new beginnings can sometimes be frightening; one can experience positive and negative feelings at the same time (for example, if one eats a food that is too spicy, but delicious—like chewing on an Elf scorched by dragonfire)--and one need not consciously acknowledge enjoyment in order to experience it.

There is a very classic human lie: "This hurts me more than it hurts you". It's not that this statement's inevitably untrue, it's that it's at best presumptuous, and at worst either ignorance or malice. There's no reason to assume an understanding of relative pain. So the one who extends suffering to another with the certainty that the inflictor, not the recipient, is having a more negative experience...is someone who very strongly wants to believe it. After all, to think otherwise would be to suspect yourself of sadism. (Or to grant room for the other to perceive that sadism in yourself.)

You can have all the very best inner buttons pushed, feel the kind of glow for which the most devoted hedonist would die, and perceive it all as strictness, austerity, responsibility, and the solemn, emotionless experience of just doing your duty. Why not? If you're really convinced of a particular worldview, what's going to seem more likely to you—that enacting said worldview means something other than what you believe...or that the feelings you get when you do the thing cannot *possibly* be counter to what you actually say?

Simply put: You can do bad, feel great, and heartily believe you feel awful about it, and are seeking to do more because you are just that damn fantastic.

It ain't deep, humans.

Of course, the Chosen One has a more specific rationale for her belief that the things sent against her are sinful: they're trying to kill her.

Yeah, she has to realize that I'd like to end her days before she can end mine, but few people meet threats to their survival with, "Well, I dislike this, but it sure is a logical response."

Poor Chosen One. Left home and hearth, set forth on a perilous quest, probably going to die.

*Welcome to my world. You know now quite a lot more about how it feels to be me.*

Welcome to self-doubt, danger, unpredictable magic. Welcome to constant attempts on your life, and perpetual tests of your will.

Oh, and welcome to secrets. That voice in your head, the bad influence? Strange thing to have inside a Chosen One, isn't it?

Dark whispers? You might think it's my voice. Only—it sounds like your *voice*, doesn't it? I'll let you in on a hidden truth: It *is* your voice. I don't even know for sure that it's a thing yet--I'm just guessing it's there, because I know altogether too much about what this quest does to one's head.

You'll find, if you aren't soon killed, and are wise enough to begin studying magic yourself, that spellcraft can do a lot of things, but it can't get inside your psyche unless you permit it to. And even then, it's pretty much only in dreams. Brains are messy suckers, resistant to forced entry. There may be theological implications here; I suspect it's part of your astral anatomy.

Specifically, I think this barrier exists due to the nature of the soul. Those things are strangely vulnerable to demise; certes, you can *murder* a soul fairly easily, just butcher the body. But you can't really influence one's inner spirit with magic. Souls are hardwired into the nature of the Universe. Each is a specific and solid Name, one that is both *distant* and *distinct*. Those are actually quite unusual qualities; while magic is not easy, most things in the Universe (even other stars) are, metaphysically, fairly close, and fairly ambiguous. Everything has (or will eventually be given) at least one name, which is, in turn, how the Universe is expressed–through a very long Name, made up of uncountable trillions of other Names, spoken slower and with more resonance than anything you can imagine.

You alter a piece of the world by drawing it to you (or drawing yourself to it) and affecting the meaning or understanding of its Name.

So something hard to approach, and with a cognomen that is quite difficult to alter, is almost impermeable. It's most famously thought that Gods alone can meddle well with souls; but it's also quite visible just how often even that appears to be a horrific mistake.

Thus: the thing in your head? That's *you*. My own voice sounds a little different. You might hear a bit of it while you sleep. If that sounds sinister, don't worry. I promise not to sing.

(I do not consciously seek to get into the dreams of the Chosen. It's just that, if you progress far enough that your life's path and mine might cross–which is, much as the Wizard would deny it, a rare occurrence–my errant thoughts will stray in directions which might picked up by your slumbering head. It's part of why I write to you; I know you won't receive these things in the way I write them (I'd be unsurprised if my most carefully-chosen words end up being some kind of nightmare about a duck) – but I put thoughts in order for the sake of both some kind of legacy of my own, and the sanity of my own skull. It's one of the ways I cope with the knowledge that someone actively seeks my murder, and is willing to commit any number of murders of smaller things in order to achieve it.)

There are dread signs and portents o'er the land. Granted, the definition of "portent" is pretty vague; almost anything can be a portent, if correctly perceived. Did you know that a two-headed calf was born in a neighboring village? Well, okay, it only had one head, but that's HALFWAY THERE.

As for the world becoming a stranger place, welcome to another secret: The more you look for the Wyrd, the more it finds you. And *these are dark times.*

Not to be confused with the 'light' times before my rule: Feudalism. Slavery. An extraordinary lack of medical assistance. Disparity between rich and poor as literal as a castle with a drawbridge and a moat.

How tempting the light. One can hardly imagine why anyone would chose the dark.

# A Tale Of The White Wizard

The White Wizard's campaign tour—that is, his gathering of al-lies—is going well. You'd think they'd have noticed that two differ-ent "Chosen Ones" died and were replaced along the way. Or, re-ally, if you look at the allies, you see why they wouldn't; they're pretty excited about polishing their swords and making sure their eventual portraits catch their good sides. They don't pay much at-tention to the kid in the robes.

It's a standard evening of overly-romanticized discomfort. The party of adventurers is encamped in the woods, despite the fact that there's a perfectly good inn about three miles back. But no, it was necessary to press on into the forest against the backdrop of twilight. (I realize that the Wizard knows I have an ability, albeit limited, to observe him through a scrying glass, and sometimes, I'd swear that bastard is *posing*.)

There they are, having just cooked some animal which never did them any particular harm, and now the White Wizard is regal-ing the assemblage around a campfire, changing the flames into shapes to suit his stories, and telling tales of history and bravery and anything except knowledge which might be even vaguely use-ful.

This is an ancient world. It had old, forgotten Gods; places which sprang up, flourished, ruled, and sank beneath seas and volcanos; beings which visited from planets inconceivable. Once, it is said, Dragons ruled here; how then did Man ever come to power?

There's so much to tell, if you know it and want to share.

That's a big "if", though.

Most of this world is not very literate. This is little surprise, when the primary source of reproducing a book is to sit a monk at a table and tell him, "Do you see this scroll? Your beard is blond now; copy it until you're grey. And then, we'll get you a new scroll."

But the knowledge of Wizards is vast. We read languages our species was not meant to speak; we have heard words from mouthless things; we can tell a history by the motion of the moon, and a future from the flight of a bird.

Why, then, does the Wizard say so little of meaning?

Why does he so seldom teach anything of practical value?

Why does he drop nothing but little crumbs?

The companions know very little of me, but they know almost as little of him. Hints and rumors, mysterious suggestions, bits of myth and legend—nothing more. How old is he? How did he come to be what he is now? No-one knows.

(Actually, I do--but they're not likely to ask me.)

Why so many secrets?

There's a flash of the dramatic in most powerful conjurers; really, if our fellow humans were of no interest to us, wouldn't we set up castles in the sky and have little to do with our previous bloodlines? Even those of us who don't actually want to accomplish something on this plane (and I'm not one of that number) tend to be surprisingly available to humans, enough so that ordinary magicians have people knocking on their doors at all hours saying, "Behold, I have found this magical locket; what are its powers?" or "Come quickly, dread demons are emerging from mirrors", or "Are you satisfied with your current flying broom? Don't be! With our new, improved, deluxe design, you could be soaring through the air like an ancient Greek about to get his wings melted!"

It's bothersome to most spellmakers to live among human things when most of us want to be left alone to research the supernatural; but we feel compelled to do so, for various reasons. The White Wizard has a sense of drama, and I—well, I have a pressing need to speak and show, as might have been noticed by now.

So that's part of playing it spectacular and yet unrevealing. If no-one knows quite what you can do, or quite what you know, then setting off the right spell at the right moment will strike rather deeper than if your fellows saw you, say, consistently levitate as you travel.

(Or if they saw you spike their drinks—but that's another tale. I see you, O Wizard.)

We try to know others through what they tell us, what we see and hear, and what we know of their history.

The White Wizard has let us know exactly as much as he wants us to know.

That's more than a little ominous. Why cloak everything in obfuscation? Why must so much knowledge reside solely in the wizard's head? Consider how dangerous it would be if some passing troll cracked open said skull.

(But that never happens. In fact, when danger's near, the Wizard seldom is anywhere in the vicinity. Peculiar, right?)

He's a grand teller of tales, our wizard. Beguiling and compelling, he weaves chronicles of ancient times as if he had been there. As if he were some ageless figure, filled to the brim with the wisdom of centuries, but much too modest to talk about it. It's as if everything were predestined, and he could impart pieces of needful understanding in the right moment, to be opened like presents at precisely the right time. It's a very pretty story. Except the Universe is not predestined, nor built around the timing or convenience of anyone. And it ain't quite so pretty a story when you start counting all the bodies.

Stories are the trees of a forest. Some assist each other, passing nutrition from one plant to the next. Some are symbiotic, living off of each other in mutual assistance and hunger. Some actively compete—race towards the sun, winner gets to spread out and grow, loser shrivels in a haze of missing photosynthesis. The White Wizard's story seeks to be the Great Tree, the vast and extraordinary oak which has been the center of the forest for millennia.

If he wraps himself around the Great Tree long enough, maybe he'll be seen that way. Because who wants to be known as the kudzu which clings to other foliage, fast growing, opportunistic, prepared to smother that plant and move on to the next one before most of the rest of the forest has had a chance to change the color of its leaves?

Don't worry. It's all part of his great plan. Everything will be fine. What's a little bit of missing information, or withheld knowledge, or flat-out lying, in the grand scheme of things? After all, this is the White Wizard. You need to do what he says, and you need to listen hard if he deigns to tell you anything.

There's Good. There's Evil. There's no excuse for condoning Evil, and no excuse for talking to it, hearing it, or letting it live.

The White Wizard embodies all that is good and right in the world, according to the only authority he permits a voice—namely, himself.

If you can't trust the White Wizard, who can you trust?

*And now, and now, there comes the White*
*Gorgeous in its purity*
*Frustrating in its barking blight*
*Maddening in its surety.*

# THOSE WHO WANDER

My dear Chosen One, it's oft-said that not all who wander are lost, and that is true. There is much you can learn by going where the mood takes you. But that's because the learning process isn't always about getting to a particular point. It's frequently about figuring out how to pull meaning from any place in which you find yourself.

But if you're going to achieve something of meaning, you're likely to need to stop, focus, and apply your will to some specific thing or things.

Were I, not the White Wizard, your teacher, this is the lesson I would give you first: Yes, there are those for whom the pleasure of the journey is its own reward.

Which is fine. For some. But not us.

Again, it's not that journeys have no import of their own; you can learn much from any path, if you have a mind to. Think of the Eight of Wands.

But keep moving long enough without a focus on the destination, and your own footsteps become hypnotic. You can circle 'round as you age, until eventually, you die in the tracks of your own boots.

You journey alone; the Wizard has left on one of his innumerable disappearances (do you suspect, deep down, that you're not the only one? It's true; he can recruit two or three others in the time it would take him to guide you properly, and he has the advantage of knowing he can replace you. He's in a particularly comfortable inn right now, while you try to figure out if this endless cavalcade of trees and beasts ever stops.)

No, not all who wander are deceived, besieged, discomforted, or at the risk of their lives.

But all who wander are lost, compared to those who seek and find destinations worthy of the journey.

I watch you. I know that you want path's end, not out of cowardice, but for the same reason that you took on the mission: there is a thing that needs doing; you are one of few who might do it; and so you will, or you'll die trying.

This is my drive as well.

I'll ask the Moon to light your way. You may die; but at least you'll die headed in a direction that has meaning.

# THE OBJECT OF DESTINY

*"You must find it, and you must use it to destroy the Dark One. It is the only way."*

*"The only way? Really? You do magic. We live in a world of gods and demons and legends. How is it possible that there's only one reasonable solution to this problem?"*

-Conversation between a certain Chosen One and the White Wizard

Why does the Chosen One need to find and wield the Object of Destiny in order to defeat me?

It's quite convenient that the White Wizard can't be the one to use the thing. Sometimes he claims it is because the temptation is too great. That is, he says that if the object were his, he would become too powerful and run the risk of becoming me.

That is not true. He's not afraid of becoming me.

He's afraid he will try—and fail.

It doesn't hurt that the road to powerful magical items is paved with good intentions and hideous deathtraps. Does our Mighty Wizard take them on? Not ruddy likely. He sends his Children's Crusade—pardon me, his Chosen One(s).

But someday, Our Hero will acquire the object. One of these days. And once the Prophesied Nitwit has the thing, we'll conveniently leave aside the question:

*Why does she need it?*

When pressed—when, against all likelihood, someone around him asks for a logical explanation—the White Wizard will often squint importantly and say that it's Balance. The Powers could not let so great an evil into the world without imposing some limiting factor. Therefore, I must have a bane.

Or else it's 'because all evil contains the seeds of its own destruction'.

Balderdash. No, no, no, no, and, just in case I'm not clear on this, no. The risk of catastrophic crash is inherent in all systems. The mark of most circumstances is not flawless victory, but the many losses, great and small, which beset any attempt to bring something new into the world.

Dark Lords do not spring forth into existence fully-fledged made for their position. We start as human as anyone. To truly reign through strength of will and force of arms, you'll have needed to risk abject failure. Most likely, most realistically, you'll fail—at least once, perhaps several times.

If you haven't gone through that process, you're unlikely to have the strength to defeat someone who has.

And this is why The Chosen One seeks some magical toy to defeat me: because she needs a crutch. She can't do it on her own. Even though the task is simply to destroy—far easier than to create—she still can't win without supernatural aid.

Which brings up a point. Another thing about that curious engine, whatever it might be – sword, gem, book, wand

(heart)

– it was created by someone else, not the Chosen One or the White Wizard.

It might have been my own thing, in fact. Study the lore of worlds like mine, and you'll find the idea is extraordinarily common: you need something the Dark Lord made to destroy the Dark Lord.

There's narrative symmetry in that, and to be fair, life often has precisely that kind of proportion. (Humans are pattern-finders and pattern-makers. Seeing the world as having a plot arc is both a way we impose our model onto the Universe, and also a normal response to the fact that the Universe itself has a beginning, middle, and end.) Ergo, "Use the evil thing to kill the evil thing" makes a great deal of sense.

But that is not all of it—or, in magical terms, that is an insubstantial Naming. It speaks about a truth, without ever getting to its marrow.

I make things. Forming Orcs into armies is not simple. Governance is not simple; even among humans, it often leads to a culling of the pack. Finding extraordinary magic is not simple. To do what I wanted done, I have built much that simply didn't exist before I was here.

The White Wizard is good at smashing stuff. That's a part of why he doesn't teach a lot of lessons; lessons grow things, and growing things is far more difficult than dropping an epigram or two and letting someone else find meaning in them.

He has so very little to offer the world. Except my death. Which is why he speaks of it so often. as if it were a bargaining chip Because as long as everyone is certain that my death will end their problems, then my killer is going to be a hero. That's you, little Chosen One...and the bearded greyface standing next to you, his hand placed possessively on your shoulder.

So you don't have my learning, you haven't gone through what I've gone through, and you expect to defeat me? How will you do that? You'd need to use something crafted through years of patience, time, hard work, trial and error...

.... Yes, something of mine.

Because nothing of yours is enough. It's not your fault. I barely know you, and I won't, if this next patch of Orcs kills you.

*And they come, in strange Orcish silence, as the Moon is but a crack in the sky; when else? Sharp daggers, and there are many of them. Arrows, arcing towards the encampment, and the White Wizard casts no spell to turn them back; I can hear him shouting, "To arms!"—but you are small, Chosen One, and bodies are fragile...*

You didn't ask for this; after all, you are the "Chosen", not the "Chooser". Most of the Wizard's toy soldiers are eager, excited, and gullible, not really capable of knowing what's going on themselves. They take this on in the hope that it will be best for others, and perhaps with a faint hope that it will change their own lives a little. The most likely life-change, for you, is cessation.

Because if the White Wizard cared much about the lives of most people, it seems to me there are a whole lot of diseases he could've cured, a whole lot of legal systems he could've reformed, a whole lot of technology he could've improved, if he was going to put his time and energy into making a better world.

But his future is a negative one: it's the same world, minus me. If that means it's minus you as well, that's fine with him—he'll just replace you.

# A Deeply Fictitious History Of Whatever This Place Is Called

---

*"We speak now of the True History, the One History, the Secret History of the world. Ignore all the other histories you have read, for they are all lies, written by the corrupt. Why else would we have burned them all?"*

- "History of the One World", author unknown

It appears as though The Chosen One had made it through a particularly nasty part of the Dark Forest. That's a bit farther than usual; good for her.

(The last three or four Chosen Ones died here. But it would be tedious, and possibly depressing, to recount just how often that happens. Suffice to say that after some interval, a bright-eyed moppet made it through against deeply unlikely odds; I salute you, kid.)

(No-one tell the poor thing that she was part of a piece of simple math: Send enough youths in, and eventually, one will get lucky enough to survive. It happens once in a while. Not often, but then again, there's no shortage of potential Chosen Ones, which is why the giant spiders of the woods are so well-fed and healthy.)

The Dark Forest is a fascinating place. It's got an odd overabundance of overhangs—ordinarily, trees compete for light and fill particular ecological niches, with those who lose out either staying small, or dying out. In the Dark Forest, they've never really stopped competing. I don't know where they get the nutrition, but they all fight towards Helios, branch tunneling through branch. They all seek to drink deep, roots gnarling into intricate underground patterns, all seeking even the tiniest wells, the smallest patch of solar energy.

They say the forest is cursed, and that's an area where I've a bit more knowledge than most. There is a trace of magic, yes, but not enough to account for the strangeness of the place. There's not a hex on the woods itself, no fell force drawing nether beings, no gateway to the unspeakable realms. Whatever spellworking happened here, it was something much smaller than would account for the sheer, aggressive murk of the place, and the ferocity of its inhabitants.

**I have a theory**: A long time ago, someone cursed the trees with a touch of ambition.

That's all. They just have a *little* bit of will. None of them is willing to die, to wither, to be smaller, without a fight. And so they keep pushing; it's the damnedest thing to see trees engaged in a rat race. They're not quite sentient, and so they just shove and struggle, even when it's to their own detriment. For example, The Great Oak of the Woods, knobbly and massive and, to our eyes, malevolent in its appearance—the Great Oak is not actually a sorcerous thing, I think. It's just a plant which would not accept its place, and kept impelling itself upwards until it had risen above the others.

Something akin to that has happened throughout the whole verdant mess. Thus the blotting-out of the sun, and with it, the coming of nightkind, those beings who dwell in curious dusks, seeking this forest because within, they need never hide from the day.

It's a peculiar habitat, an ecosphere with just a touch of magic.

Do you want to know a little about this world? It's startlingly similar to other worlds, in other universes, where humans came into being. Certainly the flora and fauna have undergone an otherwise staggeringly parallel evolution. It might best be said that this place is pretty much like most Earths, except that magic is more pervasive here. And, of course, the Gods care a whole lot less just how visibly they've screwed with us.

You see, our Gods were not content with theologically complex notions of morality. No, for reasons of their own, they chose to embody Good and Evil in the unlikely and poorly-suited form of individual sentient beings.

Or so we're led to believe. It seems a bit...weird. In a space and time where Gods have been known to walk the actual land, why would benevolent deities permit the development of someone like me? Sure, standoffish, faraway divinity might be out and about, engaging in plans beyond our ken. But our Gods tread where we tread, and run hither and/or yon, chasing virgins of assorted varieties and sometimes turning them into showers of gold and so forth. So that's not it. They're not faraway watchmakers, they're meddlers in the here-and-now. And if that's the case...why not *stop me?*

I can think of plenty of answers, but none of them are reassuring. If I actually represent Evil, did the Gods simply set me up to fail? Were the deities of Light and Dark too damn chicken to battle themselves?

Who thought it would be a positive spiritual development for human beings to divide up into easily-classifiable sides rather than to inspire vigorous debate over the meaning and consequence of our actions?

Leaving it up to humans seems convenient, but it also seems dangerous. I don't blame humanity for being flawed; without our mistakes and weaknesses, our problems and our uncertainties, we wouldn't be very good at exploring the Universe. But letting greater questions of Good and Evil be answered by humans means that you potentially run aground on some of the stickier truths of our species. That's not a thing Creators should allow to happen, if they're trying to develop some semblance of order.

Oh, it's useful for the creation of spectacular myths. Once you have decided that something or someone is really, terribly bad, then getting rid of it becomes a heroic act, and the difficulties that protagonistic persons encounter only serve to season our regard for their courage, determination, and other theoretically laudable qualities. . From there, it's a reasonable step to figure that you, as a real person, could *also* be a hero. But you run into a wee bit of trouble when you attempt to replicate that journey in the real world.

Being a hero *in an epic* is all about mighty deeds and mighty acts and just general mighty mightiness.Being an *actual* hero is about doing difficult things in spite of unpleasantness, discomfort, unlikely odds and potentially horrible consequences. It is notably unrewarding, and frankly often unpopular, since trying to do "real" good means questioning, not just the beasts who are slaying villagers, but the villagers who act like beasts.

On the other hand, just *feeling* like a hero for destroying something is *terribly* easy. It looks great. It feels great. It just doesn't always *do* great.

Consider the way the options play out. Want to come and slay the Dark Lord? Difficult, difficult, difficult.

But. Decided the old lady across the street has been secretly poisoning your laundry? Want to take her down? It's *quite* easy. And, if you have a certain mindset, it feels *awesome*.

"Burn the witch!" will always be a simpler option than, "Raise a very, very large army, cross the abysmal hellscape, battle an opposing very, very large army, and try to figure out some way to kill the Dark Lord!" And it's significantly more efficient to chant, as well.

Oversimplifying your ethics is a sure sign of underthinking.

Societal fabrics are easily torn, or, more accurately, easily soaked in oil and tossed onto the flames you're using to roast that unpopular neighbor. It's part of why good governance is not generally a moral question, but a practical one. Draconian force is frustratingly high-maintenance, and it breeds corruption and petty tyranny, both of which are bad for your bottom line. On the other hand, if you don't have some kind of approachable leadership and some sort of legal system in place, people will invent their own, and they'll do it the way any fledgling culture enacts justice: really, really badly.

Humans will be humans. That's not just a statement of fact; it's also a curse. That's one thing upon which the White Wizard and I both agree.

Deep, dark secret: The Gods, or Forces, or Powers, didn't make one of us Good and the other Evil. He and I are both products of a long series of evolving events and actions, some of our choosing, some otherwise. I'm not saying I'm *not* Evil; I'm just saying that we might need to pause and think about what, exactly, that means, and what "evil" brings to the world.

The one who poisons a friend to steal her tie? Evil.

The one who slays the High Priest of This because the High Priest of That told him to do so? Good. Or maybe evil. It depends on which High Priest you liked better.

It's not as simple as the White Wizard makes it out to be. It's not simple at all.

Why would the White Wizard lie?

Ah. That one IS simple.

If he can convince you sufficiently that I am simply pure Evil, you'll never give me a chance to tell you otherwise.

You'll never question his narrative. Not even if you're independent of thought and mind—after all, what greater service can you perform than to choose to follow Good of your own, totally unencumbered free will?

This is why you search for that which would take free will—any will, life itself—from me. One cannot permit an abomination to live, after all. And if that abomination is damnably hard to kill, so much better—so much more the glory.

Do you wish to cover yourself in glory, Chosen One?

I wouldn't, were I you. It feels uncomfortably like molten butterscotch.

# Diary of the Chosen One: On Eradicating Evil

This has been an extraordinary learning experience.

I mean, I thought I knew how to swear before. But my companions know words I'd never even imagined. I may have written a few of them down while pretending to study my runework.

The primary upshot appears to be that the Orcs are ugly, murderous rabble, and should be eradicated altogether.

I have not helpfully pointed out that my companions are some of the ugliest, most murderous rabble I've ever seen. Oh, they tend to only slaughter those who are attacking us. Or those who might attack us. Or those who might tell others that they've seen us. Or might side with the Dark Lord. Or might look like they might, if given the chance, someday, side with the Dark Lord.

But it's perfectly fine, because all of those beings are bad.

I asked the tall one with the big sword how we figured out whom to kill. He said, "It's easy. We kill the evil ones, or the ones unduly under the influence of evil."

I then asked, "How do we tell which ones are evil?"

He replied, "Those who oppose us. Those who might oppose us."

"But what if they fight because they're ignorant? What if they might not intend to fight us at all, like that weird tribe in the woods? We barely have a language in common; what made us think they needed to die?"

He gave a rich laugh, one which I imagine has charmed the garments off more than a few people, in the safety of some ballroom somewhere. "We're saving the world, champ! Saving every single living thing. That's a lot. The needs of the many outweigh those of the few, and the majority of those who come up against us are surely potential threats. If a few good ones die by accident, that's unfortunate; but we can't spare a handful of potential innocents if it means letting a score of the guilty survive. Mark my words, most of them will kill us, if they can."

My expression was quite neutral when I said, "Do you think they'd be less likely to try to kill us if they didn't know our default was to kill them?"

He smiled then, and patted me on the back hard enough to leave a three-day bruise, and he laughed again. "If they were really not our enemies, they'd lay down their weapons when we approached."

This is what I did not say: "The last time someone did that, you took off their heads as an example to others who might oppose us."

This is what I said: "I think it's bedtime for me."

I heard his following "Sweet dreams" long into my nightmares.

# THE DWARVES AND THE DEEP

Long are the memories of the Dwarves, short are their tempers. Of their intelligence, little is said, and they like it that way.

Human legend generally states that Elves are magical; Orcs are monstrous; Goblins are imaginary; and Dwarves–Dwarves are, perhaps, dogs who can talk and wield axes. They are notably gruff, presumably to hide their hearts of gold.

I've eaten Dwarven hearts. They have about as much meat as anyone else's (save Elves–those are uncomfortably like eating dust.) If the metaphor is intended to imply that they are secretly good-natured beings whose rough exterior hides gentle souls, then whoever said that is an idiot. If the metaphor's intended to mean that a Dwarf would absolutely trade a fallible fleshy organ for some kind of efficient metallic device, then we're getting a little closer to the truth.

They say I once enslaved the Dwarves. This, I did. The time they spent in my forges was not pleasant for them. They emerged burnt, scarred, and with stories they don't ever choose to tell.

They also came out with skills and secrets which had been lost for millennia. They don't speak of that, either. And they've kept those things for themselves.

They say I took their best and brightest captive. It's not precisely a lie. Those brilliant minds and extraordinary hands toil for me still. The Dwarves tell others that I keep that remnant in chains which have neither lock nor key, and this, too, is not untruth.

What can a Dwarf expect, if she labors a lifetime in the mines? To make the things of her forbears? To raise children like herself, who do as she did, whose sweat collects on the anvils of their families, whose lives could not easily be distinguished between that of today and that of a hundred years ago?

From *my* foundries emerge machines never seen before, which do things no other tools or weapons might achieve.

Dark magic? Forbidden knowledge? Sure. That, and beer which sets the skull to fly, potions which fling perception open wide, and endless words, as we take our ale and meat, about the properties of metal, the challenges of the Forge, the integration of the known and the never-tried.

They are captives of that by which I am likewise ensnared–

Purpose.

It is both slave and Master. I am not ashamed to bow my head to it. This is what we share: we will tear open the world and make a better one, or we will perish in our own inner fires.

It's a good life. It's the only life.

As for the rest of the Dwarves? They meet even now in councils of war with Men and Elves, readying themselves for the assault on my keep. Who can blame them? Going against the will of mankind is a rapid road to extinction.

Few know that better than I.

# PART II: SNAKES, SNAILS, PUPPYDOG TAILS: IF YOU KNOW SOMEONE WHO IS MADE OUT OF THESE THINGS, RUN!

## WHAT IS A DARK LORD MADE OF?

This most recent Chosen One seems different to me. A little less struck by the wonder of it all. A little more inclined to go off on her own and practice the White Wizard's runes in the forest. This one will bear watching. And that means it's time to think a bit more of the future.

Which means a consideration of the past and present. (Unless you are the sort to skip over those tedious details and move forward to your inevitable victory. The problem with that is, your victory is likely a whole lot more evitable than you think.)

So. Basics. What am I?

First off, contrary to popular belief, I'm as human as you are. One of us should probably be ashamed of that. I'm not entirely sure that it's me.

I mean, my soul is some kind of twisted, blackened ruin. But you'd be surprised how many ordinary human souls end up that way after only a few decades of life, and they're not generally doing it *on purpose*. Mine has had rather longer to cook, and I may have put a little more work into mechanizing the thing and bending it to my will—but, truly, is that worse than slowly letting it degenerate through time and apathy, as most people do?

The path of the Dark Lord is strewn with betrayal. But the Dark Lord isn't always the source. It's just that people like me are slow to believe someone would do you immediate harm in a way which ultimately hurts their own goals. It's counterintuitive; isn't longterm success, not short-term pettiness, what's valuable? Still, we figure it out. How often must you be betrayed before you see that others are taking your kindness for weakness, your silence for an inability to speak?

To make a Dark Lord, there is death and there is sacrifice and there is always, always pain. But this, too, is true for many humans. It comes down to a series of decisions: Will you turn aside from the hard path, or will you set your feet on its sharp stones?

Will you risk being broken by forces far bigger than you? (You'll never find the strength you seek by facing only the small things.)

Are you ready to fail?

The Chosen One is often told that failure is not an option. The Dark Lord knows that failure, like hurt and harm, is one not simply an option, but one of many companions. True power seldom comes without risk. Sufficient risk eventually results in harm. If you think you can trap a thousand demons and never have a single one break through your defenses and wreak havoc on your mind for a while—then you've likely never summoned any demons at all.

(And if you've never been fueled by inner demons, by daemonic passion, then you've achieved less than you might have otherwise.)

Can you achieve puissance without the hubris that will lose it? Can you lose it and claw your way back to where you were? Can you face the grief of knowing that it will never quite be the same?

There is no truly powerful magic without danger. Play with danger long enough, and being damaged, being broken, becomes essentially a mathematical certainty.

This isn't simply mystical. This is true of almost every worthwhile human endeavor. If it's always easy, then it's quite possibly never, ever really meaningful.

One of the Chosen Ones will eventually make it to me. But that One will not arrive unscarred. Because you simply cannot get where I am without taking damage. I couldn't; no-one else can. The same math that says, "keep throwing Chosen Ones at my defenses, and eventually, one won't be killed" also says, "...but the odds of making it here without some form of physical and mental harm are vanishingly small."

Shattering is easy. Putting back the pieces is not, and there are always some parts missing. Forever.

And you have to know that, and understand it, to get to where I am.

Consciousness is hard. The death of a beloved dog is sad for both master and pet; but the dog's ability to understand what it is losing is tremendously smaller than what the master will feel, when it comes that person's time to die. We face a knowledge of mortality, pain, illness, diminishment, and possible future horrors, in a way that nonsentients simply cannot. Trees don't really understand when the whole forest is ablaze and about to be turned to cinders; humans can get a tiny burn on a single finger, and from there they can extrapolate, think about, even feel what it would be like to be burned alive.

(And relatedly, this is part of why some cultures make the burning of witches as public as possible. Sometimes they say, "It is so all may see justice done," but most of the time, they mean, "Now you see what we can do to any who oppose us. Or consider opposing us. Or who simply cross our paths on the wrong day." Theirs is a strange belief system, one which permits you to think that someone is a magic-user with both motivation and ability to harm others, yet which feels you can roast them without consequence. Either you must not truly believe in their magic; or you must have a deep belief that you are protected by your own righteousness.

Be careful: certainty in your own righteousness is a disease which leads to symptoms such as blindness to the world around you, inability to truly see or hear others, and gaining an unhealthy pleasure from the unhappiness of others, predicated merely on the idea that those others are 'wrong' and you are right.)

How do we deal with the fears, the challenges, the difficulties of sentience? Sometimes, we shut off as much intelligence as we possibly can, live mechanically, fail to think, or adopt cultural or personal ideals which try to eliminate self-examination.

The rest of us? We suffer, and we go on.

We all know that the Chosen One suffers. She does so, not because it is dramatic, but because the journey is difficult and painful. The Chosen One most likely to succeed is the one who has come closest to the struggles of the Dark Lord.

Because the will to power never comes from a place of idleness or ease. Power that is merely given or inherited is worth only a fragment of that which is paid for in loss.

Whatever the Wizard lost in order to get where he is, he lost long ago. But the Chosen One? She bleeds afresh as she picks out another history, pieces together another fragment of the past, gets a somewhat closer look at who she is, who I am.

Sometimes I send a spell or two for her to play with, attached—because I am a traditionalist—to the pecking beak of a crow. She's figured them all out—and made friends with the crows, dammit. I'd resent that, except, rather than simply send the avian things off on their way immediately, she tends to point them at the White Wizard, to see them take a stripe or two out of his face before they head home.

It's a tad adorable.

# THE LAW OF SACRIFICE

It seems to be a common belief that one becomes a Dark Lord in order to have everything. But that isn't **possible**. To give just one example, you *lose* some of whatever peace you might have had, pretty much right away; you can't achieve power without also calling the attention of those who desire, fear, and envy it.

*The Wizard and the Chosen One have traced my backtrail through a particularly secret grotto today; the Chosen One solves a riddle I'd hoped was rather more impenetrable. The armies of Man and their allies train relentlessly, with that singleness of purpose unique to angry humans given sharp toys. I re-cover my scrying stone; staring too long at your upcoming demise is tempting, but unhealthy.*

I am reminded now, more than ever, of the temptation to leave all this behind, to work towards being the monster they say I am, to stop having human cares. It's quite achievable, and there's plenty of precedent. Traditional methods include such-time tested methods as altering the body deeply enough to change the mind, self-directed soulectomy, or simply delving so deeply into the secrets of the Universe that your brain stops thinking on a mortal scale.

But *there's no sense in working with the world of sentients if you're not going to relate to them as sentient.*

Oh, there's much you could do if you chose to just break human minds and use their bodies as tools. If you know sacred geometry, if you understand hidden architectures, you can erect structures to alter the motion of stars and planets, warp the flow of time, devise any number of changes in the Universe. These things are really done more efficiently by acerebral slaves than anyone else; as a technology, throwing a century and a hundred thousand lives at a pyramid is fairly effective, if you don't care in any way about the potential of that time or those lives.

It'll get you a pyramid, but what will you have lost in terms of all the other things humans invent and develop, when given a little time and opportunity?

Those who don't measure opportunity cost are destined to have fewer opportunities, and ultimately, no matter how grand your schemes, that makes for a tinier world.

This is why, contrary to popular belief, I have no desire to rule over "everything." My reasons are, I might note, perfectly practical. After all, how much control can you *really* have? How much focus do you *want* to put into making laws, and then carrying those laws out through scrying and enforcement—rather than spending that time in the study and practice of as-yet undiscovered magic?

And for that matter, why would ruling, itself, be an objective in the first place?

Sure. Power is intoxicating, and its own reward. But power itself dilutes all too easily. Is conquering another country an increase in power, or increasing the size of potential rebellion? Is appointing new lieutenants an ability to delegate more and focus on tasks only you can do, or is it opening the way for others to feed off of both your success and (presumably) your citizens? (You could spend every moment watching your lieutenants; but that involves giving up ruling for being the equivalent of a theatregoer. And I can assure you: the dialogue is *terrible*.)

And again: leave a people insufficiently governed, and they are unlikely to simply adopt some natural utopian state. There are few things more boring, in my personal opinion, than overseeing some kind of judicial system. But there are even fewer things more *ugly* than the Mob, which is born when you permit people to avoid that bothersome due process thing, and simply let them decide who's guilty based on how they're feeling that day. And mobs destroy things, both property and person, *of whom and of which you could have made something useful.*

All right, then. Let's say you love death for its own sake, and thus revel in the opportunity to perform great demonic acts by conquering larger and larger populations and offering them up to the Dark Gods. I won't deny the allure, nor the rush it brings. But woe betide you if you pollute too much of your headspace with that addictively blissful, narcotic feeling. Woe again if you run out of victims; Dark Gods are not plants, which wither when you fail to feed them. If they hunger, they'll come find you.

If your personal pleasure is seeing a mountain of corpses, bear in mind: enslaving yourself to pleasure is a fool's path. Using power to get what you want is natural; forsaking your *wants* in order to fulfill larger goals is strange and (perhaps?) inhuman—but it's ultimately the only way to get where you want to go.

(Speak to me of necromancy? That's a specialized art. All power seeks to claim you; that is one power which will do so faster than you can run. It's not hard to generate potency through the last gasp of an ended soul, just as it's not difficult to create darkness by snuffing a candle. Show me someone who can enlarge a soul, though, and I'll show you someone who can make the shadow leap from the wall and tell you truths of things unseen.)

That being said, your opponents lead nations; it's probably wise to have one of your own, unless you want them to go straight after *you*. Best to have your own sovereign country; they won't acknowledge your sovereignty, but they'll still be formal about declaring war. Nobody wants to start a precedent of "invade when you feel like it"; they're too vulnerable themselves.

So you must govern; and you can't govern without ever hurting anyone. Show me a monarch without blood on her hands, and I'll show you one who's never ruled. Politics is a clean, happy, positive business under only the rarest circumstances. Democratic rule? Everyone thinks everyone else is an idiot. Despotic? Everyone wants to overthrow you, either to install democracy or to be the next despot. Kingdom full of abundance? Someone wants a bigger share. Kingdom starving? Someone needs to find blame.

It sounds pessimistic, but it isn't. The basic motor of human progress is *discontent*. The fact that humans always find more things about which to be discontented is not a problem. The *problem* lies in the many unconstructive ways they choose to express and attempt to exorcise their discontentment. For example, it's easy to make politics into a game of getting good at politicking, rather than good at governing. It's easy to go to war and think of all the land you might conquer, and downright damnably difficult to consider, much less replace, the resources exhausted therein.

Also, some people don't like it when they make corpses, even if those corpses are wearing very snappy soldier's uniforms.

The truth is, everything in the mortal world is made to fall apart. The only way to truly fight that is to bring something new into being, and to do that, you need to wrest Creation right out of the screaming, endless maw of the Void. To do *that*, you need to sacrifice yourself—your energy, your sanity, your possibility of being like others. You need to feed the Making Machine out of your own veins, *or it just won't happen.*

This is the law of sacrifice: You cannot have all things. You must give up some of what you might do, have, and become, or you will have nothing. Those who believe they have everything? They're deluded. Don't tell them—the poor fools are probably happy.

This is a lesson in creation: The first blood of blood magic is always your own.

*Blood for the blood god?*
*Never known*
*Not when your veins are richly sewn*
*With fuel you can use to tear the world asunder*
*The blood god will simply have to hunger*
Sweat and tears? Yes, in great measure
*Change the Universe. Truest pleasure.*

# DIARY OF THE CHOSEN ONE: FRIENDS

Friends help you move. Real friends help you move bodies. True friends help you move the bodies of those who turned out not to have been friends to begin with.

I'm not sure why the Dwarf is helping me—oh, we've killed together, we've buried a man together, and still, he prefers to be "the Dwarf". He likes me, I think, but not enough to give me his name.

What fool tells his name to a dead girl, after all?

I think the Dwarf knows some of what's going on. I think his people sent him here to die. I get the idea, vaguely, that he is being punished, or else he is some sort of royalty. Which one, it doesn't matter. He's meat, and he knows it.

I can understand him, sometimes, when he speaks his own tongue. It's surprising how quickly I seem to pick up languages. Perhaps I've always been this way, and simply wasn't around enough words to realize it. I've been seeking to understand more things ever since I was old enough to realize The Secret: there was knowledge being withheld from me because I didn't know the code. Each realization came in turn: that the code was everywhere; that the strange patterns painted on a few signs and gathered into books were, in fact, bits of information; and that the town drunk both could read, and might teach you if you could steal a few coins on her behalf.

That drunk also sometimes, in her cups, sang in a tongue that didn't make sense. Eventually, I got her to help me understand those sounds too, and this was likely how I first figured out that what I was speaking wasn't "human", but just "the tongue of where you are right now". I thought then that I was lucky to find such a person, but it turns out, as we voyage through more hamlets than I knew existed, there are a few really learned people in most of those places. There's rather a variety: people who studied under some Wizard and were released; former nobles, disowned by their families; itinerant bards; custodians of long-gone libraries. All of them drink. All of them avoid the White Wizard. Which is why I seek them out after he's supped, drunk, smoked, and fallen into that state of log-shattering snore factory he calls "sleep".)

(I think the White Wizard has a few words for educated people who disagree with him, and those words are "monster", followed by "corpse".)

The Dwarf, I believe, thinks that he is teaching me just a few words of Dwarfish, as one might kindly assist a tourist with phrases like "Where is the bar?" and "This bar is out of whiskey, where is another bar?" But I appear to be picking it up more rapidly than I ought to know words.

It's weird. But what about this whole situation is anything else?

This is what the Dwarf says, every night. Quietly, and in Dwarvish.

"Dark is sleep and dark the mines
Dark the heart
Opalescent the dreams.
But thunderously bright
Burns the mind which drives the hammer."

# CARE AND FEEDING OF GIANT SPIDERS

If your average massive arachnid is a bit needy, bear in mind that in some places, if they're large enough, they're worshipped as gods. It seems quite a step down to go from mass exultation to hanging around in the dark, waiting for adventurers.

Or perhaps not. It's an odd life for a preternaturally vast Araneae predator to be a pet. And that is, after all, what being a Spider God tends to be about. Consider: arachnids and humans can't really talk. So the relationship consists primarily of the humans bringing food to the beast, in the hope that the beast will bite the sacrifices, and not the supplicants. (I'm also sure that Spider God priests have entire theologies based on the idea that getting their congregants eaten is for the 'Greater Good'. Count on it.)

This "worship" may or may not involve a cage—but even without one, it feels quite a lot like domestication.

Even if your creature is of a variety which prefers to stay principally in one place and wait—say, a vast version of something from the Ctenizidae family—she will, nevertheless, prefer the ability to roam, even if she doesn't use it.

After all, *freedom isn't how far you choose to go; it's whether or not the choice is made for you.*

The truth is that giant spiders are unpredictable, in ways that even the largest of their normal-sized brethren are not. Arachnids are often somewhat larger than their prey, but most of them consume insects, which are disproportionately stronger than, say, mammals of comparable mass.

But grow the arachnid tremendously, using magic to circumvent some of the pesky limitations of biology and physics--and suddenly it is not simply a dominant predator.. It's now so much more *unspeakably* powerful than most of its food that it's *ridiculous.* A human who lifts twice as much as has his body weight is very strong; an ant which can only lift ten times its weight would be incredibly weak. The giant beast has gone from ensnaring things its own size or bigger through cunning and literal webs, to essentially having helpless soft things thrown into its mouth. That's *got* to be weird.

If I raised dogs instead of wolves, I'd expect them, eventually, to obey without question. You can teach them that, now that we've domesticated them. But wolves are not that way at all. I'm not sure that I could train them not to chomp me. If I could, I *wouldn't*; I'd rather assume they might sink their jaws into anything they choose, and they and I ought each keep a respectful distance in general. I'd hate to take away their strength simply to gain their obedience; what good is it to control a thing if you have to destroy it to do so?

Likewise, you can't really drop a giant spider into an artificial habitat and expect it to thrive; you can only create environments where they *might* thrive, and hope they choose to stay. It's hard to plan around the desires of a free creature. That's *damned* inconvenient. You might wonder why it's worth the effort.

Until the creature faces off against slaves—like dupes who don't question their ideology before they stake their lives upon it. Then those True Believers find out just *how* hard a beast will fight in order to remain free.

# DIARY OF THE CHOSEN ONE: I HAVE FOUND ANOTHER DIARY

We got out of the forest, and none of us are dead. Small blessings.

Today, we witnessed some atrocities. We came to a village, burnt beyond recognition for some crime we'll never know. All we know is, the Dark Lord's troops were here; it's their bootprints next to the great piles of cinders which were once buildings.

Smashed buildings. Roasted humans. I don't know what happened in this place, or why. I wish I did.

The Dwarf was quiet and grim tonight. He pulled out a flask, and handed it around. Whatever was in it tasted a bit of apples, and a lot like swallowing the lit end of a torch. It was good.

We were quiet tonight. We'd seen a lot of death. The others had picked at the rubble – found some supplies, a weapon or two.

I found a diary.

Or something similar. It's not like mine. No words. Just illustrations.

Orcs. Some sort of winged thing with a horn on its forehead, half-glimpsed, nature unknown. And the White Wizard.

And one great battle. The battle is beautiful, even though I can tell that it's basically just a scribble to whoever made this. There are details I wouldn't even see, much less think to draw. But that's not what really matters. This is the only part of the little book which has words. They're crude, as if letters did not come easily to this person.

"All dead."

The body beside it was about my own age. Looked a bit like me, to be perfectly honest—stand us next to each other, and someone might think we were distant cousins, perhaps. Or just friends who'd spent a lot of time around each other.

Not that the diarist will be doing any standing, unless someone raises her from the dead.

The wound is clearly from an Orcish blade; I can tell, because the blade is still sticking out of her. But I suspect it wasn't done by an Orcish hand. This is no particular feat of deduction. It's her own hand grasped tightly around the hilt.

So I am not the first. It's a little bit of consolation to know I was right.

And I'm not the only one who's thought of that particular exit from this story. And that information...is no consolation whatsoever.

Onwards. There are still plenty of lives to be taken before this is over.

"Saved". I meant to write "lives to be saved".

# THE WAR-SONG OF THE ORCS

Orcs.

They live underground, deeper than Man ever delved. Their tunnels are hewn with strange shapes which form (if you follow them, mile for winding mile) peculiar and curiously semi-repeating patterns which change depending on which paths you take, and which make a sort of music when air gusts against them; an art much more intricate than any cave-painting.

All Orcs are raised for battle. Was this always so? They have histories of a time before Man, but few sing them. I have never heard even a line of those tunes. Only a few elders know them, keeping them safe until the day when they matter. Because they speak of something too painful to be mentioned casually: *sunlight*.

Human lore says that Orcs fear the Sun, hate it, are even caused physical harm by its rays. That is misunderstanding, or propaganda. It is more true to say that daylight makes them cry with longing.

This is the war-song of the Orcs–loosely translated into human speech:

*We are the people.*
*We are of neither night nor day.*
*Both are home to us, but only in the night are we permitted.*
*One day, one day*
*We will rise. Our children will see the sun without fear. But first,*
*We will make sure we are never driven back into the night again.*
*Those who would see us trapped underground, they will fall before us,*
*Because neither conscience nor memory will permit peace with those*
*Who forced us into blood and screaming.*
*And should any survive,*
*We will leave them be. Because when they take flight*

To our caves,
They will not survive.

Man is not weaker than the Orc, nor is the underground full
Of terrors he could not surmount—save one.

Give Man no enemy to fight, and in a single generation beneath the surface,
He will turn on himself.

We are the People. We are of neither night nor day.

We have lived underground for ages past counting.
Every day in the dark is a chance to make our knives sharper.
Every sharpened knife brings us closer
To cutting through
The barrier of night
And seeing Day again.

# Unicorns: Sparkling with Hate

It's a little-known fact, but Unicorns are something like 20% paint, and their horns are stolen exclusively from endangered species. Yes, Unicorns can, indeed, sense virgins and do, indeed, approach them. For one thing, they're fully aware of how embarrassing it is to have a quadruped reveal your sex life.

There are plenty of legends about what they were like, once, but the tales are similar to legends of dragons, in the sense that they're totally unhelpful--though for precisely opposite reasons. Dragons have no real desire for humans to know them, and did not, for a long time, consider it worthwhile to change what humans might imagine. By the time they realized the consequences of this, there were far too few left to tell tales; and those who remained considered "conversation" to be perhaps the twentieth response to human approach, somewhere after "flame them very hard" and "flame them much, much harder".

(One might speculate that dragons would need to be at the edge of death to speak to a human. And most humans really would not *enjoy* that conversation.)

The horned things of legend–mostly magical horses, though I've seen quadrupeds of all varieties–the Mythicorns have been part of things nobody should ever have to experience, back when the sight of them inspired instant terror. Horses are wild, but they're herbivores, and they don't think the way sentients do. A being which looks like a horse, but eats meat, thinks, and carries a grudge is...*difficult* for humans to handle, particularly when you believe, for some reason, they want riders. (I can assure you that they do not.)

Their lives were not pretty, and though we called them beautiful when they were possessions, sentients feared them once they got loose. Consider an intelligent horse who has figured out gelding and decides to try it on others. That's when we saw that they seemed to be some sort of frightening parody of the animals we'd domesticated, and we considered them ugly.

They don't want to be viewed as ugly anymore. One way to do that is to become beautiful.

Another is to make everyone else feel gross.

What were they like? I don't know. They've spent much time having those with hands write down their stories. The tales claim that their shiny exterior mirrors luminous, loving hearts.

Fairytales lie. Especially, especially when told by Faeries.

I'm quite sure there were dissenters. Piece together enough histories, and you'll realize that many Unicorns seem to die offstage, to leave the heroes rather suddenly, never to appear again. The sagas mention that they passed in tragic fashion.

But Unicorns do not bury their dead; they leave them in middens. The bones found in their places of worship, central to their habitations, are decorated with stones, sometimes with precious gems.

The oldest Unicorn habitats, now abandoned, bear a curiosity for those who make a careful study. A bit away in the forest, outside of view of the village, there'll usually be a smaller collection of skeletons. *Those* have no ornaments to mark them, but they show a curious commonality: they've all been chewed. By sharp, equine teeth.

# A Dark Lord's Lullaby

*Every childhood nursery rhyme*
*Echoes in my head*
*Everyone I knew back then*
*Wants to see me dead*
*Sleeping potion by my side,*
*Demons guard my gate*
*At night the dark embraces me*
*An always-faithful mate.*

When I was a child, like many children, I believed there was a monster in my closet. I was frequently told this was pure fancy. But with what I now know, I realize it was quite true.

It's still true, in fact. But I'm not afraid. I've also learned that there is a greater monster in my mind. *And that matters more.*

You can destroy the monster in your closet easily by refusing to believe in it. There are many things of magic which will just vanish if you don't put a puff of imagination into them.

So we're active in withholding, in withdrawing, that belief. We often don't want those things to lurk in our rooms and dwelling-places.

But if you end that closet-creature, beware! Because in so doing, you also end a part of yourself which is capable of seeing things which are not wholly there. Not for most people, at least. And so we walk through existence, blissfully blind to both daemons and doorways.

We give accidental and murderous life to our own shadows, sometimes...with the same tools we use to raise up cities out of dust.

Imagination is not an easy tool, which is why so many reject it entirely. Others think to pen it in, to keep it in place, to hold it down--as if they could choose which pieces of humanity to embrace and which to reject, without costs. As if they could have the ability to perceive far beyond the visible sky and into unknown worlds, without also catching glimpses of the long, cold void of Space.

The Multiverse is vast, and not all of it is friendly or pleasant. But some of the most difficult places are some of the most important to experience. One's skull is not necessarily meant to be a perpetually comfortable place; brains are shot full of zooming electricity for a *reason*.

# Diary Of The Chosen One:
# Dwarves Revisited

Odd creatures, Dwarves.

Some of my reading suggests that in ancient times, if the children of Men were deformed, they would be sent to caves. It is explained that they were changelings, wrongly born to human mothers...or perhaps some sort of genetic cuckoos, finding their way into alien stomachs in order to grow.

(Did you know that the beautiful cuckoo bird will push other eggs right out of nests and then steal the nest? So the Ranger told me, in one of his more helpful discussions on the nature around us. Granted, he then said, "And that's why we can eat any damn eggs we find, kid! If the birds don't care, why should we?")

(I wonder if the Dark Lord thinks, "If they don't care about each other, why should I care about them?" But I imagine those are treasonous thoughts.)

If you're looking for the remains of ancient libraries, moldering texts, and bits of cryptic knowledge, I'm guessing there's not a better place to be than on the hunt for the Dark Lord. Because she passed through here first, and we are, to some extent, backtracking her long-ago trail. She was clearly intent on plundering the knowledge of now-vanished Mankind to enslave its future.

Or else she really, really likes the smell of old books. If so, she's not alone.

There isn't much written record remaining of why people are the way they are, and I had never heard of "anthropology" until I'd bought a considerable amount of whiskey for one particularly squirrely itinerant scholar. I remember the conversation quite well:

"The goal of anthropology is to study mankind and try to understand who we are and what we do."

"That sounds difficult to quantify."

"I can assure you that, having done a fairly thorough examination of the data at hand, it is, in fact, quite simple: We're a bunch of right bastards, we are."

Still, if you know that the study of humankind exists, and you find yourself encountering its lore and knowledge in all manner of secret places while you attempt not to get killed, you can learn a great deal in a short time. You have to, I think; learn today, because you might die tomorrow.

I'm no historian, no expert at anything, really. But I pick up what I can. There are few sharper motivations than the knowledge of your own likely cessation. In that regard, I'm not sure why I don't spend all of my time with a sword, trying to fight better, instead of spending just enough time to be adequate, in between what appears to be abstract philosophical study. The sword seems like a wiser and more measurable thing.

Only—what we are going to encounter is obviously, visibly, far more than what could be handled by a warrior, or a hundred warriors. Maybe an army, maybe two, but not an adolescent with a sharp pointy thing.

I may not know where knowledge will take me, but if I can figure out enough, synthesize enough of the information that's pouring in, perhaps I can also figure out how to survive all this.

Or I could just count on the White Wizard for knowledge.

(I'm not sure what the Wizard knows, but the list of what he doesn't know is pretty vast. I'm pretty sure that includes my name.)

I've studied what records we have of prehistory. Older lore says we were giants once; but I doubt it. I've seen Giants, lumbering past, and they didn't attack us; they walked away in mile-destroying strides before we could get our act together and shoot them. Seems distinctly unlike human behavior on the part of the Giants; our little band is probably not be difficult to squish, and we're surely enemies. If the Elves were huge, there's no doubt the landscape would be littered with bits of once-thinking roadkill, crushed under vast Elven boots.)

But some of the other knowledge seems a bit more solid – ancient scholars believe we lived in caves, based on crude paintings on the walls and the position of human remains. They believe we found the Gods late in our development, and that is why said Divinities meddle little in our affairs. And scholars have written fairly extensively (as much as there's extensive writing on anything) about shamanism, because it led to the magics of the modern world, this fast-paced, futuristic realm where there are sometimes more than three or four copies of some of the most important books, and carts can travel at a breathtaking four or five miles per hour.

There have been other Dark Lords; not many, but some. It's hard to tell, but I'm generally of the opinion that the shamans of earlier Man believed every tribe had room for only one twisted mutant. And they didn't want the competition.

Dwarves claim to be part of the brotherhood of Humanity and Elves. Elves tend to insist on it, in fact. This is because Elves love their fellow magical races, and has nothing to do with the fact that even my cursory, amateur reading of Elven holy tomes can tell that they devote significant segments to short jokes.

(They also consider both combs and mirrors to be holy objects, and state that the Mandate of Heaven falls upon "That One who Hath the Highest of Cheekbones.")

I do wonder about Dwarves.

The Dark Lord is mentioned in a few of the relatively recent myths. It's said that certain tribes of the Dwarvish people were forced to forge strange objects for that dread being. Dwarf lore speaks of "enslavement", but at least one hand added, in the margins, "to large portions of mutton, and barrels of mead".

It's an odd joke.

That same source also speaks of "a night of terror with the Dark One, from which many mighty warriors emerged with their skulls split in two", but we run into the difficulty that the Dwarven word for "mortal wound" is nearly indistinguishable from the Dwarven word for "hangover".

One thing's sure: the Dark Lord definitely has an army of Orcs. And Dwarven hatred of Orcs is legendary.

Also fascinating—since they both live in the Underdark, and there's that famed animosity, you'd figure they'd be at constant war.

But that doesn't seem to be the case.

Perhaps this is because they fought wars of unimaginable brutality at the dawn of human history.

If they did, they don't talk about it. Or have records of it.

Perhaps it was too abominable to want to remember.

Much like this quest.

# THE MALFORMED

Dwarves are the only beings of Light to live underground; a strange circumstance. (And that's from the perspective of one who literally *makes* darkness, but habitates aboveground–rather far above, in fact, as my keep is on a mountain and my chambers, as is both traditional and strategically reasonable, are in a tower). Likewise, we think about Dwarves engaging in a constant struggle with the other inhabitants of the Underdark, just as I am, I suppose, theoretically at perpetual war with the assorted dwellers in sunlight.

But as any student quickly learns, there are no real records of this fissure-bound conflict. Or if those records existed, they've been wiped from the chronicles, long before my time. Dwarven histories actually seem to have a bit of a taboo when it comes to Orcs. They call them "the Malformed".

There are two things which are peculiar about this. One, it is the same word Dwarves used to use for the children they, themselves, abandoned–before the Dwarves were civilized, of course. They carried the small things into the deepest caves–

--and left them there.

The second thing is this: strangely enough, "the Malformed" is what, in the oldest texts, Orcs call themselves.

I have a theory here. It's about unchanneled thaumaturgical discharge.

Magic abounds in this world; it's not precisely everywhere, but it's in more corners and small spaces than you would suspect. The words of which the Universe is constructed sometimes contain force which overflows, or even spills out, leaving ambient and raw witchery in peculiar places. Sometimes it is literally in the air, sometimes it is a part of formations of trees or stone. Sometimes we craft it through knowledge, the mixture of certain terms, ingredients, and motions which call to the inner characterizations of places or things.

Now, magic is shaped (most forcibly) by will, by desire-- intentional, or otherwise. This is part of why all things--not just Gods--are given shape by the stories told about them.

It's not *quite* true that you become what you believe yourself to be. For one thing, the spellwork of crafting illusions is far easier than the sorcery of pushing matter together into a form we'd find coherent. So ofttimes, you'll work enchantment on yourself, but it's just the enchantment of seeing and believing what you desire to see. (This is so frequent in human life that even worlds which have no magic see this happening on a regular basis. Brains can do that.)

Likewise, not every thought manifests in the physical realm. If it did, the person who shoved ahead of you would be struck down in that brief moment when you think, "Hey, that place at the bar was MINE; DIE, you bastard!" Our heads prevent most of those thoughts from escaping, thus preventing hurricanes of mystical backlash. That's one of the reasons magic is so difficult to learn, and also why it's much easier to build a chair with wood and saws and nails than by trying to think it into existence. (And if you want a good solid wooden chair, that's your best bet; as much as you can, work within the confines of what you can see and touch. If you want a throne carved from a single diamond, you'll *have* to re- sort to sorcery and alchemy in large doses. And then naïve reality will fight you every step of the way.)

But there's very little thought more powerful that the communal mind – it's why group ritual was both the first theatre, and the first magick.

(It's also why I decline to be worshipped as a God-Emperor; be- ing the focus of so much psychological force is never good for keeping your ego in check, and why inflate egotism when it's a known weakness of Dark Lords? Even if you can control your heart and forebrain, being the focus of the mass mind makes you shine like gold, and it inspires the covetous to try to take that shine for themselves by stealing your throne–or life.)

Speaking of stolen lives:

Begin with something human. Now put it in the lightless places, and tell it loudly that it's *not human at all*. In so doing, you start enacting a most powerful hex, one that's hard to resist even if you disbelieve it yourself. (If you're already open to the idea that you're something broken, if you already believe that in the deep wells of your own consciousness, then everything is exponentially harder.) Being irradiated by the by-product magic of the world, and inculcated with the hatred of those closest to you, you will surely mutate. And thus: Dwarves from Humans. Or so I believe.

Now, Dwarves remain *part* human. Which means that–for a while, at least, until they rejected enough of humanity to be free of that particular disease of the *homo sapiens* mind–they did unto others more than was done onto them. For 'round and 'round goes the wheel, and if you don't work to break a cycle, you begin to reinforce it. You breed your own bane: Orcs from Dwarves.

And thus: endless wars in cold, unlit rock, fighting like hell to gain...cold, unlit rock.

You might think they had a common enemy in humans, but it's damn hard to hate your parents, isn't it?

There's too much pain in blaming those who brought you forth; far easier to displace those emotions onto someone close, rather than your distant family/forsakers. And so: blood, blood, blood underground. Forever and ever.

There's no way to break the cycle.

Not from the inside, anyway.

And this they sing, deep in their caverns, deep in their cups:

*Hear us, Gods!*

*We do not fear you in earthquakes, in mine collapses; those are part of our days.*

*And if you would strike us with lightning, you'll have to reach down in the mines*

*And there you dare not go.*

*You make your rules*

*We make our way.*

*We do not pray to you, we whose lives are hewn from rock.*

*Strike us down, if you will. And if you can.*

*We are too busy seeking that which shines below the surface*

   *to worry about how you glow far, far above it.*

# "If Orcs Could Talk"

Children of this world often ask, "If Orcs could talk, what would they tell us?"

This is strange when you consider that the oral history of the Orcs is older than that of humans by several thousand years. Linguistically speaking, human beings are essentially precocious toddlers in comparison. Still, I'm not surprised that there are kids who don't know that Orcs can speak. A surprising number of adults are wholly unaware of it, as well. Granted, many adults live in a state of what appears to be the most purposeful ignorance possible, but I am a Dark Lord; I may have a slightly cynical worldview.

Anyone who says there is no darkness but ignorance should spend some time in the pitch-black room that is a superabundance of questionable information.

Frankly, I suppose it's not even a *bit* peculiar that certain depths of ignorance have survived throughout human history. Or more specifically, that they have survived into *today*. Now in particular, we live in a time of extraordinary amalgamation and collection of knowledge; much as I generally dislike humanity, I can't help but recognize how well the species has done in its hunger to advance, to change what we can know and transmit. It's made fundamental alterations in how much we can affect the Universe, I think—the White Wizards have never had so much power, and, so far as I can tell, even among the rare arisings of Dark Lords, I am...unusual.

Knowledge is not, as commonly, believed, power. Knowledge is *better* than power. Power brings force and vitality; knowledge gives you those, *and* an understanding of how to use them to construct more complex and farther-reaching enterprises.

And yet:

Everywhere I go, I find burnt manuscripts. Old, cold ashes, preceding me into even the most far-flung cemeteries. It's hard enough poking through that odd collection of half-recollections and natterings we'd like to call "the past". (Study the patchwork of 'history' long enough, and you'll find that, much like 'self' or 'justice', the *idea* of the thing sounds solid, but the actual components are riddled with the most fascinating pieces of pure opinion, and the most *impossible* conclusions. It's all thrown together as if it were, say, a very small stone building, made by drunken masons, using whatever random materials they thought they could stick together long enough that they'd get paid before it fell apart completely.)

And it's ever so much harder when more than a few interested parties--friends of the White Wizard; his Order; certain Men; the Elves—have clearly been going around, crossing out what was originally inscribed, and writing new bits in, hoping we wouldn't notice. Their explanation is simple—"that was tainted with evil, and we could not let it stand." And I'll never know if that's true, of course—because I'll never be able to read it; it's crossed out, overwritten, vanished, or simply in cinders.

Uniting words through force creates a pretty narrative, I suppose, but truly, the thought of understanding the world through simple narratives is one of those ideas which becomes increasingly disquieting the more you get close to the sources. As I've said before, humans are pattern-makers; this is part of how we're so quick and bright at figuring out how to catch fish, which plants make good drugs, what pointy things remove life force the fastest. It's also how we end up with so many idiotic ideas. Pattern: Those who eat a certain leaf feel less pain. Let's experiment and see if we can lessen more pain, more efficiently. Pattern: It's important to kill mindless pests. If we assume Orcs are mindless pests, then we understand how to handle them—namely, fatally.

Even that assumes we're all on the same "team" – that if you find a particular leaf makes you very sick, you'll go warn the tribe, instead of, oh, telling a certain someone it's a wonder drug, and then making off with their mate.

One intentional untruth is a lie. A thousand intentional untruths become a worldview.

Those who are most likely to appoint themselves as gatekeepers of knowledge tend to say that histories are full of lies, which I'd say is correct, as long as you define a lie as "information they can't control".

(I don't mean to malign every keeper of knowledge—not by a long shot. If you face those difficulties, and still have the courage to write your truth, I admire you and would like to read your books.

And I'd do so, if ever I find a way to reassemble them from their charred component bits.)

In any feudal society, if you have a noble class, one that has the Mandate of Heaven—and is, thus, one that supposedly exists because the Gods gave it right to rule--it's an easy theological step to assume that things the rulers do not enjoy are actual evils loose in the world. Sometimes a general or a great warrior or the occasional scientist or inventor or architect will lament that we know so little of our past. Ah, but humans have a simple response:

"The past is lost to our use, for the Gods wish us to fend for themselves."

I, again, imagine this is more plausible in a different world, on wherein, unlike here, you seldom see the Gods hanging out near temples, playing squash.

But it doesn't matter, because now, we have an even better idea:

"The world has always paved the way for Dark Lords. Only the White Wizard and his friends can keep them away. Ask him to tell you of the past; he'll explain that monsters always ruled, but now, and only now, we have the ability to find those monsters. Rely on the keen eyes of the White Wizard. Things of the darkness tremble at his glance, for they see their destruction in his steely gaze." Omitted, but perhaps useful, note: I *do* see my destruction in his steely gaze. Because I see *everyone's* destruction in that lofty, sociopathic stare.

# THAT WHICH IS DONE FOR THE GREATER GOOD

*There is a King of Man, and nothing is good enough for him, no sword sharp enough, no battle line crisp enough, no preemptive portrait of my demise sufficiently lifelike, nothing will satiate him but my death. I like having terriers nipping at my heels. Inspires me to keep moving.*

When we look back at the history of government, we find it ain't there. Makes sense, really. Few rulers are terribly fond of the thought of holding on to data from generations past. They like the benefits of knowledge, and enjoy them when they're packaged in the form of better crop yield and sturdier peasants...but they really hate how often critical thinking forces them to confront truths that they can't acknowledge as being true. In this thing, as with so many things, nobles are precisely the same as serfs.

I'll reiterate: histories lie. They don't always lie from spite or from propaganda, or from a distrust of letting the little people know what really happened. Sometimes they simply lie because the historians themselves have no real interest in the loss of a meal ticket or a head. Particularly when the continuing attachment of the head to the body is quite pressing, and some especially unbecoming behavior on the part of the Queen's grandmother is in an enviably-distant past.

More often, though, we lose information because people simply "know" things, and therefore, nobody's going to disprove that stuff. For example, the White Wizard's companions "know" that everything an Orc says to humans is in bad faith; it's either untrue, or intended to mislead. Ergo, we oughtn't listen to Orcs; simple!

According to that utterly trustworthy and never self-deluding fountain of knowledge about humans--that is, humans themselves--there are basic things upon which you can set the bedrock of the Universe, and one of them is that Humans are Good. Oh, they sometimes do bad things, but most of the time it's just the fault of some rogue enemy tribe, and an accurate accounting will show them being properly wiped out. By the grace of the Gods, of course, who are assuredly on the side of those who commanded that a given history be made into a tome.

(Why Humans do this is obvious. Why the Gods don't object is a bit more perplexing. It's my personal belief that they decided, long ago, that humans were going to muck about with the retelling of *anything*. So the Gods adopted a philosophy of "Any press is good press", and went back to turning people into swans at semi-random intervals.)

*Because Humans, Humans are the inheritors of wisdom. They are the progenitors of veracity. They are the beacon in what is an otherwise dark, hostile and otherwise unfriendly universe.*

People like the White Wizard always go all-in on something they know to be untrue, particularly after it's been questioned. They will fight for it, argue for it, put together brilliant strings of logic for it, use every tool of academe and every tool of rhetoric, and then invent new ones, just for the purposes of making quite sure that their accounts are indisputable. Anything except *actually do what they say you're supposed to do.*

C'mon. History should be a great story of winners and losers, and, obviously, it ought to be a parabola, charting the ever-increasing knowledge, wisdom and beneficence of the human race. If events themselves do not easily lend themselves to that arc, why, then there must be a deficiency in how we ourselves see or understand that story.

As the tale of humanity grows ever grander, humans get to hold dear the sweet, sweet knowledge of being deeply special creatures. The human psyche is a tremendously complex thing and, in some ways, a tremendously fragile thing. It overloads too easily, in an infinite Universe. So it's important to give the brain a set of principles, a foundation, an architecture of rationalization with which to tackle life. Humans should never be exposed to any of the true Names of things, lest the numinous glow sear their retinas. This is part of why the White Wizards join together in mighty Council, to help humanity understand which words are acceptable and which must needs be cast out before they doom us all.

It's fortunate that they possess this cosmic wisdom; how did we survive without it?

They do have a particular advantage, in that there is nothing in the world so unbelievable as the truth. It comes, not dressed in finery, not in the careful make-up of the courtesan, nor with the honeyed flattery of the courtier. It attempts to persist through sheer virtue of the fact that it models reality in an accurate way; but who cares?

I can't say when this whole mess got started, but I can't really fault people for the way their fears rule their lives. (It's not like I am without fear; I just recognize that if it gains the upper hand in my mind, everything I've done crashes down. And I won't let that happen—not by my own hand, at least.). At this moment in the timescape, humans have no real capacity to even ponder the thought that they might've been doing things horribly wrong for years; what an existential terror that would be! Particularly once they realize that it's not in an isolated incident, in a particular moment, or under the reign of some inauspicious king, but instead—perhaps—they have been piling wrong on top of wrong in the hopes that it would eventually join together to form some kind of cohesive right.

What else could they do? What other choice would they have?

If you know you are right

And if others oppose you

Then they must be wrong.

And therefore, they need to be destroyed.

*It's for the greater good.*

When you break it down, the idea is that Good must prevail *because* it is good. That particular tautology may be a part of why logic is not a beloved curriculum in the monasteries and schools of my former people.

A little knowledge is a dangerous thing, which is why it must needs be tempered with a tremendous amount of fiery ignorance.

# DIARY OF THE CHOSEN ONE: WANDERINGS THROUGH MYSTERIOUS AND POSSIBLY POINTLESS PLACES

And then we passed through the fields of fire, and then we passed through the mountains of fire, and then we passed through the oceans of fire, and it may be a sign of how surreal this has become that the last one didn't seem tremendously more ridiculous than the other two. And then we passed back through the fields of fire again for no particular reason that I could see. And then we passed through the forest of night. Later on we realized this was a mistake and the forest was perfectly normal; We simply shouldn't have been adventuring through it at 2:00 a.m. We went to the lost archives of a lost civilization and got horribly lost. We visited and ancient Ruin which turned out to be largely a hoax invented by the local tourist industry. Every once in a while, I think the White Wizard might be stalling.

We grow experienced in our skills and we build our camaraderie. OK, I'm probably lying about some of those things. I am better at swinging a sword than I used to be. I am considerably better at reading through historical documents and doing ever-more-complex pieces of spell work. The sword part happens because we keep going places where we attack the inhabitants, and the magical part happens because I am determined to figure some of this stuff out for myself; we're steeped in magic, and I don't want to have to try to filter everything through the White Wizard. That, and I'll admit: I'm fascinated by magic. If one of the high points of my life was trading alcohol for literacy, one of the things which gives me motivation to wake up in the morning is the chance to unwrap another piece of the (admittedly endless) portions of the Hidden World.

The most enjoyable parts of my day are the ones where the Wizard slumbers and I can sit back with a wineskin and some text of mystic import. Or even better, simply wandering just far enough from the camp that I am out of earshot, but not so far that I'm likely to be consumed by the local flora and or fauna, and thinking about the power we call "Word". The great Word from which we get that designation is vast, unreachable by human minds—but also contains all the smaller ones within it. And some of those are within our grasp—or might be, if we can only figure out how to extend the reach of our minds that far.

The more I acquire even a basic education, the more I recognize that there is no grave secret to the composition of the world. Everything is made of atoms and elements and forces which all act on each other in ways that, in this realm at least, matter not even a little bit. Not unless you're engaging in something mundane, like building a bigger and better crossbow. If you are, physics and engineering will suit you well.

If you want to do something with magic, though, the real power of this world, you must needs harness Word, and Intent. You might rote-memorize a few hundred incantations and brute force some sources of power (unwitting acolytes are, historically speaking, a good way to begin) – but you won't really be getting to meaningful knowledge that way. That's the sort of childish stuff you could do after studying for, say, 20 or 30 years. Real power? That takes time. The lifespan of a White Wizard, say. Or a Dark Lord.

Which is, by my calculations, a good 30000% longer than the life of a Chosen One.

# ON THE MAKING OF NAMES

Why are Dark Lords powerful? They use horrifying, monstrous secret magic; ask anyone.

Why does a Dark Lord rise? Because so many humans are secret sinners, protesting that they want the Light while actually seeking to serve evil. *It's an epidemic. Fear it.*

What does the follower of a Dark Lord look like? Why, just ask the White Wizard. He will point the maleficent out to you. They'll claim they're innocent, but if they weren't monsters, why would they look like servants of darkness to an expert? *The White Wizard fights evil full-time; are you doubting his ability to sniff it out? Is it because you, yourself, are just barely concealing your true hideous scent? Come a little closer, into the center of this ring of the Righteous, and let them smell you. Let them inspect you for the marks of impurity; you seem to have worn your hair shaggy, like an Orc. Your shoes are fine now, but we hear you go barefoot—like a Troll. Didn't you say the word "sorcery"? Are you a Sorcerer? No? Then why are you talking about dark magic?*

Stories. They only belong to the people if the people demand to speak. And oddly, they seem to find it safest to speak in unison. Nobody wants to stand out. Sure, we burnt the last dozen who seemed different; but that's only because they were evil.

Remember, if you're good, you've got nothing to fear. This bonfire will only be used on people we know to be bad, and you're not bad.

Well, maybe you're a little bad.

Hm. We don't want to waste a good fire, do we?

In our hearts, we are all swayed by the mob. It would be a poor survival trait if your every instinct was to do the opposite of your fellows. This is why your emotions are treacherous; I trust my own heart about as far as I can throw it, which is perhaps thirty feet.

Humanity is full of change-makers; but eventually, we stop asking, "What are some of the possibilities of the Universe?" and start asking "At what temperature do people cease asking annoying questions, and is it necessary to apply the flames to the entire body, or just to certain particularly sensitive spots, to make that happen?

Even I, as a Dark Lord, see this; I see it quite a lot. I am still human myself, and I'd be a damned fool to stop watching others because I'm too "evolved" to learn from my kind. Granted, I am a bit changed by magic and by the necessities of combining supernatural amounts of spirit and will within the frail shell which is a living being. (Holding together a physical body under the strain of nearly endless mystical forces as they're channeled pell-mell through a puny human body is *not* precisely what one would consider wise. Not if one values the flesh one is using as a conduit, and prefers being a living sorcerer to a sizzling corpse. Nobody said this was the easiest path; or the smartest, for that matter. It's just *my* path.)

I seldom go into the details, but you must have gotten a sense of how betrayed I feel. How violently angry I am at having been cast out—even though, long before I had my name plucked from the Ostracon, I was often on the verge of casting *myself* out.

The ones who wish to see me end have named me Evil; and so I will take that term, and make it my own.

The great Name, of which the Universe is made, is not the cognomen of some God or even some set of celestial forces; it is Universe, engaging in a primal act of definition. As strives the cosmos, so strive the minds within it.

If we don't want to see this in magical terms, it's easily found (everywhere) in our ordinary interactions. The man who consumes a glass of wine, followed by a half dozen more of the same, may not get so drunk as he who has one glass of Skull Smasher, the homemade specialty of the house. Skull Smasher may not be some deeply potent vintage; it might, in fact, be a slightly fortified beer. Not much alcohol, perhaps not significantly more than was in the wine; but by its epithet we desire it, and through that epithet we make ourselves *certain* that we've been dosed with some potent venom, something like what the Gods drink before their great brawls. What's in a name? Every. Damn. Thing.

What we name, we thereby claim, and that, in a nutshell, is what brought us to this moment. It is humans who, more than anyone else, must see a thing and call it useful or not useful, desirable or worthy of scorn. There is so much power in Naming; even if magicians didn't know its underlying place in cosmogony, humans are clearly inclined to lay claim to the Infinite through our words.

As a simple example: why label the White Wizard as righteous? Because you seek the authority, the comfort, of knowing someone is out there, embodying all that is good, so *you* don't have to.

And if the label's not accurate, doesn't fit the thing upon which it's been stuck, well, that probably won't matter in the short-term. Except if you're inaccurate enough, you'll eventually break whatever you're working on. You can take a hunk of jagged stone and call it a wagon-wheel; but it won't travel very far.

Likewise, it's hard to turn lead into gold; it's easy to paint lead bright yellow and *say* it's gold. A good test of magic is finding out what happens when you knock it about hard enough to scrape off the shiny cover, and see what's inside.

# ON THE UNMAKING OF NAMES

The sounds of marching are everywhere in my land now, as various creatures muster around what would be my banner, if I had ever seen any particular need to have one. In one of my (very) few attempts at communication with my former cultures, I tried to warn people: *in seeing monsters everywhere, you make new monsters.*

They didn't listen to me, of course. Because it's bad policy to listen to a monster.

Here are just a few things the White Wizard never discusses: how I govern, how my system of ethics works, why I left, *what I've actually done.* This is not coincidence. "The Dark Lord" of whom they speak is not me, because it's not *anyone.* It's not a person; it's the unpleasant tingle at the back of your neck when you think you're about to be mauled by a bear. To see me as a *person* risks facing that adrenaline-fueled fear, not far away and threatening, but here, immediate, and in your mirror. They thus need to view me as outside the human race, a disaster, like a storm or an earthquake.

Bear witness: *it's they, not I, who called forth the tempest.*

This is part of why I speak so much about what I think, what I believe, what I've figured out. These are things that matter; and thus, *I care what we name them.*

It should be said: from the proper angle, I am *horrible.* I am a terror. I am a monster. I've never sought to deny it. I am a thing-once-of-the-clan, now-outside-the-clan. There is a simpler word for that: I am a *threat.*

You might fear someone before ostracism; but you recognize that you have to fear them *much* more afterwards. Because when you denounce someone, remove them from your culture, *you stop having the ability to tell them what to do.*

I am monstrous because I challenge the identities human culture has attributed to others. I am proscribed because I question humanity's supposed right, theoretically granted to us by the Gods, to assign to the Universe only the titles and ideas which make us comfortable. I am a Namer.

Naming, in human mythology, is a power not always given to the gods, but always given (somehow) to humans. *And by the power of the name are we given dominion over all things.*

Metaphysically the entire multiverse is one long slowly-spoken Name which began at creation and stretches forth throughout everything that Is. The world we know consists of fragments of that word, each one connected, more visibly or less, to those long, long syllables spoken by the process of stars and seas moving and vibrating imperceptibly in time with each other.

Amongst that backdrop, we could be readers of that word, if we study it hard enough. Some of us, like me, seek to change or even reWrite that thing.

But most seem content to let the word pass them by, never knowing it's there; living automatic, responsive lives. It's not necessary to see the word or the Names around us, any more than you need to think about oxygen in order to breathe. There are runic and mathematical complexities underlying everything we touch, but it's not required that one know the secret sounds of the World in order to be a part of it. You can simply hear it as background noise, if you choose, shutting it out.

Why not? It's safer; if you never take on the part of one who attempts to give meaning to the Universe, you have a chance to live a less complicated life, concerned only with yourself, your friends perhaps, and with the sorts of things we substitute for meaning. How often have you heard someone argue passionately that the world ought to be a different way, without once putting forth a method as to how this might be accomplished? In that frequent pastime, you see the metaphysical made mundane and expressed by your fellow man; impressive, surely? Sometimes, for extra effectiveness, they even yell.

You only really need to consider these things if you wish to use the power of primal creation to lift up works of your own, to catch a part of the Universe with your hands or mind and channel it through you. That's a difficult, dangerous matter, compared to simply holding onto the pleasant, understandable things which surround us.

The one exception to this cosmological blindness is the afore-mentioned Naming. We do it quite casually, this world-altering re-development of the fabric of Everything. Politicians, firebrands, academics—each one gets a rush out of slapping a label on a thing and saying it is Defined. And even the most grounded, unenchant-ed minds can feel the power inherent in that act. When we name things, we tell them what they are, what they will be, and what they cannot be.

Give something an appellation, and you impose upon it layers of reification; you reshape it by mutating or trimming or stretching it to fit what you want it to be. Humans do this more than any other thinking things, and by that act, we form an existence where hu-mans *ought* to have dominion. Why not? If we Name all the things, then we are the Knowers, the Shapers. We are certain that we un-derstand That Which Is. It's why so many of our belief systems add, almost as if it were an afterthought, the idea: *of course all this was made for us.*

Here's the simplest application of this as it applies to my life (and, perhaps, upcoming death):

*You create a life where you fear shadows, but you also know how to drive them back with candles and bonfires, and you keep claiming that you're just bringing light, even as the heat burns everything you touch.*

And that's the real birth of the Dark Army. That is what brought them here, those who've rallied to me. We are the cast out, made to vanish into unseen realms. But now we wish to return, and we do so knowing the secrets of the dim places. *Fear us.*

Humans have defined them as things of the Dark, and this they are forever doomed to be. Unless they can remake that definition. If they can change the definition of their habitat from "underdark" to "sunshine".

Sometimes I wonder what would happen if we simply took a de-serted part of this land, unclaimed and unoccupied, somewhere far enough from Man that it would take humans a long time to find that strange settlement. How one might seed the colony with enough works, enough agricultural tools, enough war machines, enough ideas, that by the time the humans did get around to discovering the Creatures of Shadow, sunning themselves on the beach and ordering drinks with umbrellas in them, the former beasts of the Underdark would be well entrenched. (In half my heart, I believe: humans would still breed and swarm and overrun them all, as they always have. And yet: perhaps not. Not if the will of Man was turned inwards, towards self-reflection, instead of outwards, towards crushing all that caused troublesome thought.)

Perhaps the march of the human plague might be slowed, might even have some grit tossed in its gears. I don't want humans gone; I just question their right to curate the world. Over the longterm, avoiding the ugly, casting it all into a box labeled "anathema" and forgetting it existed is *not* a good tactic. Not if you want a future, instead of an Apocalypse.

# Diary Of The Chosen One: It's Always Lovely In Elf-Land

It's a perfect day here in Elf-land. It's always a perfect day in Elf-land. They've regulated their weather so that it's exactly what they all like.

I'd ask how they all have similar tastes, but I have a fairly good guess. They say that Faeries steal human children and replace them with their own offspring, but if you've ever met any Elves, you know that's insane. I'm pretty sure what happens is they leave humans the offspring they don't like, and then the humans that they take—

You know, I don't really want to speculate on that at all.

You always eat well around here. The Elves are strict vegetarians. At least, they are when we're around. But they never let us near the kitchens...

Elves have been a part of this land for a long time, and they say they know, better than anyone, the depredations of the Dark Lord. They are, after all, a far older and wiser race than Man.

I'd find that arrogant, except that by now, I know enough history to believe that the average tribe of semi-friendly orangutans may be an older and wiser race than Man.

The Warrior of our troupe has been mooning over a number of Elf-girls. Each has rejected him in public and, as far as I can tell, disappeared with him (separately) on given evenings. I believe he is in Love. I'm not sure where that is, although my assumption is that it lies somewhere between Limbo and Purgatory.

It's so beautiful here. They live by consensus. Contrary to popular belief, there is no Elven royalty. All are equal here. We're told. There may be a Throne, but they would never fight for it; they share all things in harmonious generosity.

But really, it's weird that we're never allowed near those damn kitchens. Or the mines. Or the servant's quarters. In fact, we've never even see where those things are. We're not quite sure who clears the dishes or makes the beds or tills the fields.

"Magic," says the Wizard.

"Not important," says the Elf.

"Are those dresses really made of gossamer?" says the Man.

Nothing at all says the Dwarf. But I have seen frozen mountain-tops less bleak than the look in his eyes.

"Elves, in beauty
Shining with grace
Stab through your back
While they lie to your face."

This time of quiet has been intended to give us a chance to rest from the rigors of our journey.

But all I am is restless, and doubtful in my mind.

# THE HUNGRY MOON

This, then, is the Moon:

It is a lifeless rock, reflecting the glory of the bursting and long-lived sun. It is barren, it is empty, it holds and fosters no breath.

And yet, it's not dead. It's an antithesis of death. It's vibrant, taking in solar rays, converting them into a shape of its own making, and shooting them back to us in irresistible form.

The Moon is hungry, and she desires to have us. But she won't claim just anyone. Those whom the Moon would consume are, themselves, possessed and possessive of that flavor of madness which is irreversibly addictive. Once you're Hers, you're Hers.

The Moon infects us, blesses us, devours us. That pale wrecker, Death, is only a sad imitation of the lonely and fulfilling object (and creator) of desire which is our lunar tyrant. Longing is her nature and her trade.

Humans seek to grasp the Sun and are burned; but the Moon, having no fire, does more: unlike those who embrace the bitter solar heat, some of those who seek the lunacy can take her into ourselves and not die—or at least, not die quickly.

*This is the Moon: her language, all howls, is more musical than any human tongue. This is the Moon: no goddess, but for some, more worthy of worship than anything divine.*

This is the Moon: raining down her strange, reflected glow, giving back a measure of her own limitless hunger.

For this we thank you, O Moon:

*For making us insane.*

*For making us hungry.*

*For making us broken, to make us whole.*

# DIARY OF THE CHOSEN ONE:
# AND THEN, THE DARK LORD

Drunkenness has the advantage of blurring the world around you, but it has the tremendous disadvantage of being only temporary. It recedes, leaving your stomach sour and your head feeling like it's cracked from the inside—and then you have to handle your life. And maybe that works, if you're rich enough to buy all the wine you want, to keep making everything push back away from you. Then again, maybe it doesn't; I've met some rich people, and if they've found happiness in anything they bought, they didn't share the feeling with others.

Still, I thought I'd see if wine might bring out something useful. Maybe not sleep, but perhaps a soothing of the passage of hours. There was plenty to drink, if I wanted it. We found jars and jars of Orcish wine in a barracks. So we took it. After we killed the Orcs, each and every one of them, of course; it's them or us, right?

(I'm told there isn't an Orcish word for "mercy". Granted, I'm told that by people who don't speak Orc.

But, after all, if you can't trust your homicidal, condescending, stone-ignorant companions, who can you trust?)

(Nobody. Not now, not ever.)

I had wandered away from our fire—the night wasn't too cold, and there are only so many off-key songs of bravery you can hear before you consider putting a dagger through either the singers, or your own eardrums. And there she was. I'd never seen a picture of the Dark Lord, and this figure didn't quite meet the description in tales—being, for example, about ten feet shorter than I'd heard. In fact, I think I might have had an inch or two on her. And she wasn't cloaked in garments of ever-moving shadow. It was just an ugly tunic, something you'd work in, greyed from too many washings and stained from—from wherever stains originate, if you're a Dark Lord.

I considered the idea that it was a dream. I... sometimes hear the Dark Lord in my sleep. For that matter, I think she sometimes hears me. I like to think this is some superstition, some atavism creating a mythical connection between hunter and prey.

But I knew it probably wasn't. And I don't know all that much in the way of sorcery, but I'm pretty sure of this: she didn't open the channel. I did.

Perhaps I really wanted to know what ultimate evil was like.

Perhaps I was just sick of the company of my companions.

I suppose, at first sight of the Enemy, I should have run. Or should have shouted for help. But I couldn't. I'd like to say I was enchanted, that the being had cast some spell on me, but this is my own damn journal, and I won't lie to it. More than a few Elves, assorted shamans, and the Wizard himself have all cast a thing or two in my direction, and I'd always been able to feel it. This wasn't like those things. I wasn't held by magic.

No, there wasn't any sorcery here. Just two drunks, in a forest. The Dark Lord lifted a massive, not-particularly-clean horn to her lips, drank. "We've only a little time," she said, "before the Wizard is likely to notice me. So I can't stay." I was going to ask the obvious question, but she answered before I could speak. "Killing you would do me no good; the White Wizard would just get another 'you', and likely one with far less interesting dreams."

"Why not kill him, then?" Treachery, treachery, and I was only one drink into the conversation.

"Because I'm not sure that I can. And even if I could, it would take a lot of time and energy, and I have an empire to run. I could hurl death-spells down from my tower for months or years; but the land would fall into disarray. It's hard to divide your time between creation and destruction; if you notice, all the White Wizard does is concentrate on destroying me. It's why he's relatively good at it. And it's why he's never done another damn thing, nor could he if his life—such as it is—were in the balance."

I don't remember The Dark One's words exactly, or mine. I'm probably writing them down a bit better than they sounded, on both sides. I think there was a certain amount of coughing, and hiccupping. Apparently, hiccups don't humanize a Dark Lord; you can sort of feel the power coming off that oddly-human creature, and realizing just how much force is inside something patently human is actually more unpleasant than watching it issue from some sort of golem or daemon. It's disturbing to see that the Dark Lord is still human.

At least, if you've been around enough humans, it's pretty disturbing.

The Dark Thing passed me the horn. I think I tested the waters, said something dredged up out of my rote lessons—though not before a considerable swig.

"Not to be argumentative, but I'm pretty sure that evil needs to be destroyed."

She gave me that smile again. "Evil's an idea, not a thing. I worry a lot more about those who want to destroy ideas than those who want to destroy things. Although I don't really trust either one."

"That sounds like exactly the sort of platitude someone would want to use if they're trying to excuse evil by discussing its nature."

The look she gave me should have been frightening, I think. If it wasn't a look I'd felt on my own face, at least a few times.

"You're not wrong, but you're still missing the point. How do you defeat 'evil' if you don't decide what it is? It's like saying you want to 'defeat a mountain'. Do you mean that you want the hard work of climbing it? If so, how much help will you accept? Would being guided by someone who's already ascended the mountain take away from your 'victory'? What about being teleported to the top? Is the victory in the climb, or in attaining the summit? Or do you mean something else—like taking an army of workers and some alchemical explosives, and hewing a road through the mountain so that it's no longer an obstacle—and maybe no longer a mountain?"

I shrugged. "You are a literal threat to humanity. Do you deny it?"

The Dark Lord, Bringer of Ever-night, Scourge of the Boiling Seas, laughed. Her laugh was hoarse, bitter, but also very real.

"And what is the White Wizard, then?"

"He's intent on saving humanity."

"Well, thank the Gods. No ill has ever come from that, eh, Chosen One?"

"So you're not evil?"

The creature grinned; they had infectious eyes. "Haven't we talked about this in your dreams?"

I looked at her sharply. "If it's really you in my dreams, how the hell did you get there? And also: GET OUT."

Now the grin's gone.

"You invaded my dreams first, my little Chosen Child Sacrifice. I've done enough that deserves blame; don't put your own shame on me. I wouldn't mind having a more private head, myself."

I sat back. We both remembered the alcohol at the same time. The robed one took a swallow so long, I wondered if Dark Lords had a spell for drinking. Or maybe just a lot of practice.

"So you came here to turn me? To make me trust you? Because you can't, you know."

She didn't answer for a moment.

"No. Not to trust you. To see you with my physical eyes, instead of sorcerous ones. Very few of the Chosen have made it this far, you know."

I couldn't help it. I asked, "How far have my...predecessors gotten?"

"The remnant who got to a place like this one gained at most another two or three weeks into their journeys before...before the Wizard found it necessary to make replacement."

"So this is a tunnel? We all go the same way?"

"No, this is a world, Chosen, with vast and untapped possibilities—still. There are some things that everyone has to do; you need that thing you're going to get, the one that can kill me."

She held out the horn. I hesitated. "Why should I trust you? Who knows what potions you've put in here?"

"Who knows what potions the Wizard puts in your daily bread, Chosen? Ultimately, you can't know for sure that no-one is deceiving you. You can only seek the strength to throw off deception—by others, and by your own heart. But your own studies, such as they are, have to have shown you that there's no potion which really enslaves the will and leaves everything else intact. If nothing else, that's not what magic would want. Magic is fueled by will; humans abnegate their own will often enough. Magic would never choose to poison the very soil which might see it grow."

I shrugged.

"And besides, you can see a little bit into my heart, as I can see into yours. Damned if I know why. But I couldn't come here with intent to poison you or trick you. Not from this close. If you make it, we're going to fight, and one of us will die, but not now."

This was the logical moment for me to ask why the Ruler, the Beast, was really here, what she wanted, what the game was. But I didn't want to. I was curious as hell about this creature, this thing for which I had travelled untold miles and weathered nameless hurts.

I took the horn, and drank.

"Why do you do—what brought you here?" I asked.

"Love of humanity," she replied. I choked on the mead, splashed it on my face. I didn't care; her comedic timing was perfect. I resolved to practice telling a few more jokes. Before I could admonish myself for thinking such trivia, she added,

"I was imprisoned, and no-one freed me.

I cried for help, and no-one freed me.

Eventually, I shook off my chains and I returned.

They said, 'Why do you no longer love us?'

I said, "I realized that you have always been my chains."

I nodded. "The story of the Djinn."

There are many stories, and many Djinn, but she knew the one without asking. "Exactly. Imprisoned, she is so desperate to leave that that she doesn't think about the cage, because to do so is to begin to despair. She focuses instead on the one who will let her out. For the first hundred years, she thinks only of how she will reward her rescuer with great wealth. For the second hundred years, she thinks she will be so grateful, she will give her rescuer with power over the world."

"And for the final centuries, she thinks of only one thing: how much she will hurt whoever frees her, and then, all others, everywhere." I finish the story for her. It's been on my own mind. The Dark Lord nods.

"I have no intention of punishing the world. I won't be that djinn. But I will never, ever let them put me back in the box. They'll have to kill me."

The Dark Lord looks my way, and I should be embarrassed—I am the weapon which will kill her. But I am not ashamed. I have my purpose, and what would be shameful would be taking the simple way out, would be failing from lack of effort instead of through opposition. The Dark is said to be seductive, because it is easy, or because it is forbidden. Not true. Dark is seductive because it is almost what we are. It is very nearly us. It is a few choices that we make or don't make. It's not a line that we either cross or do not; it is a series of cracks in the ice of a river, and it's the difference between skating past, or staying static and falling.

We both drank more. And we spoke for a few minutes. Of absolutely nothing important. Afterwards, it's easy to think of how much I should have asked her, what I could have tried to learn, what weaknesses I ought to have probed. I know I stayed, telling myself I was seeking vulnerabilities in an opponent.

That's not untrue. This is the Dark Lord, and it needs to die. Needs to be killed, specifically, and that's my job. The Ruler has to be destroyed because it will help. It will make things better. For people. Which is noble. I'm certain of that.

I think.

I don't remember when we parted. I don't remember if the cloaked one vanished into a puff of smoke, or turned herself into a speck and caught a ride on a passing bird, or if she just walked away.

I know I slept pretty well that night.

I may have a mortal enemy. But I don't feel so alone anymore.

# Brewing a World

*What has countless thousands of legs and only one angry mind?*

*A centipede, or a mob.*

*The Army of Man is vast, well-equipped, ill-tempered, and full of cannon fodder, a thing I find impressive, since no-one on this plane has invented cannons. I hear their boots stomp ground in unison; it's my own personal death-knell. I don't like it, although, to be fair, the beat is catchy and you could probably dance to it..*

*But they've a long way to go to get here, and I've much to do before that happens.*

The Gods did not make humans and then place them each, immortal and perfect, on individual desert islands, to live out the lives of monks. They made it easy for us to die and kill, and then put us in close proximity. We're *meant* to be around each other, we're *meant* to affect each other, even if we don't *like* each other. It's not necessarily essential (defying what we're "supposed" to do can be a rewarding vocation) – but it's silly not to recognize those inclinations in ourselves.

Personally, I think you can't get farther from being an island unto yourself than to be a maker of maleficent magics, living in a fortress keep. Here I have a realm's worth of strange things known and unknown, creeping out of darkness underground, walking upright in the shadowy alleys and sidestreets. I'm self-contained, and yet, I am quite connected to the world. The world and I have a deal: they won't stop talking about me and my supposed crimes; I won't stop remembering to make their lives unfortunate.

Disconnection is no virtue. I am quite certain that if I simply turned my back on everything, pretended that I was never an ape, I would end up, not in some glorious postmortal state, but simply in denial.

If you were that human, isolated on the aforementioned island (let's make it a desert island for an extra note of inhospitable unpleasantness)--perhaps you'd have to make up a cosmogony centred around the existence of only one sentient, a solipsism of comfort. Even then, I imagine you would talk to yourself quite a lot, and in so doing, you'd make an "other" with whom you debate.

(That's assuming you'd already learned language before being placed on that island, of course. Otherwise, you might simply go feral, be without words, be without the ability to name things. But then, you would not be a part of the same humanity as the one that has words. Maybe you wouldn't be a lesser thing. Maybe the rest of humanity might be the lesser thing; mortal words represent only a fragment of the world they describe, and one might argue they're part of the problem of being human. But if you're a beast and not a Man, then you're outside of my scope; speak your truths to wolves, for they are nearer kin.)

When I was first taking up dark magic, one of the clearest goals was to be immortal and unkillable, which, I felt, would make everything ever so much easier.

It turns out that if there's any way to make magic do that, I can't figure it out. I still look from time to time, because who wouldn't, really? But the Universe abhors stasis, and making yourself into an unchanging, undying thing is about as stuck in place as you could possibly get. I've lived quite a lot longer than I would have otherwise, of course. And it is quite difficult to end my life. But it's very *possible* to do so. More than I'd like, certainly.

I don't want to die, which is why I still chase immortality, but aside from the technical problem of, oh, the Universe resisting with extinction-level force when you go up against that particular part of natural law, I also recognize that creating endlessness in myself would come at the expense of many of the other things I want to create or have created.

That is the thing for *anyone* who generally moves through time at a consistent rate of an instant every instant: the use of your limited time is the measure of what you are. The distribution of your hourglass-sand is *important*. One of the most critical steps towards self-definition is the choice of how to invest your passion. Because it's one of one of the temptations of sorcerous power, let me remind you again: *Immortality dilutes urgency*, makes it less vital that a thing happen in this place and at this time. It makes you less likely to create things for the sentients who are, now, just mayflies to you. It's *hard* to make deadlines when your checkout time is "never". Contrariwise, it focuses the mind something *fierce* to know you've only got an hour or two left.

*Art and creation require attachment, not avoidance.* Making something involves connecting, even if you connect in a negative way, even if you arouse anger or pain or fear. If it is to be meaningful, it *must* mesh with the tellurian and if you are to connect with humanity, regardless of how you feel about that horde, or how it feels about you, then you *cannot* be immortal. I need to be able to end, because I fervently want to create meaning and I know, if my back's to the wall, I absolutely *would* die for that.

I know that even more now that the possibility of said extinction is close at hand. After all, The Prophecy—with the help of the White Wizard—has been bringing about an exciting shiny new Chosen One every time the last one takes a dirt nap. They've been getting closer and closer, and this latest one is, admittedly, particularly extraordinary. The odds aren't good. Statistics are not generally on the side of Dark Lords, especially since our plot armour tends to have a big giant hole in it saying "Insert Protagonist Here".

# But then, Magic Really Wants To Kill You.

There's not really such a thing as "White Magic", and if there was, it would be no more forgiving than any other sort. The kindest priest of healing in the most compassionate temple in the land...is nevertheless engaging in hazardous activity with each curative invocation. If all he knows is a simple healing spell, just a *little* tiny one granted by a superior, passed down for generations, known to be safe, well understood—even with all that, nevertheless, magic, disruptive by its nature. dangerous without exception, seeks to pull free of any binding. Healing someone more rapidly and effectively than might be possible without sorcerous intercession? Seems benign. But what if you heal the wrong person? The eternal struggle of What Might Be picks sides pretty easily. You could end up sworn to Law or Chaos or Broccoli with extraordinary swiftness. Because, as noted earlier, it's not like magic *itself* thinks about these things. And the kinds of divine forces which *do* keep score have neither time nor inclination to check everything out. They'll just sort you into wherever's most convenient, and go on looking for more worshippers or making new planets or whatever it is they're doing with their time this aeon.

Meanwhile, there remain many people, even on this world, who don't know what magic is, or who fear it. Actually, there may be more magical skeptics *here* than in worlds *without* magic. Anything which might make your neighbor unfairly more powerful than you ought to be viewed with a certain suspicion. Have you met your neighbors? They're *terrible*.

(Some of them, anyway.)

Then there are people who really won't accept the idea that you've healed someone out of the goodness of your heart. They might make the very, very human choice of believing that the unnatural has struck and that where something is unnatural, it threatens them, regardless of the form it takes. (They're not wrong; I don't think they're wise, but they're not strictly incorrect. Unknown powers are a threat; it's just that if you destroy all threats, nothing ever gets a chance to become assets.) They might deify you. Or they might kill you. Or, again, going back to the general history of humans, the pattern is often to do the first, then the second, and then do the first again.

What have I done with my own magic? Less than I would like, given the time I have left. But I've made a few things I consider worthwhile.

Over the past several decades, I've raised up great circles of stones, a feat of magic which was remembered for about one generation, after which people started saying, much to my annoyance, that the great monoliths had "always been there".

I'm not the first to do this sort of thing; not by a long shot. And I'm certainly not the first to choose to make enigmatic monuments with meanings that are astrological, runic, metaphysical, and historical. But I would like to think the ones I built are unique in at least one way. The megaliths are, like many such things, made to align with certain configurations of stars. The difference here is, mine don't match the stars in *our* sky.

I have built foundations for cities, diverted water, changed the nature of soil, altered some of the ecology of a particular place as best I could. It is remote from pretty much any habitation, but it could house a population of thinking beings, should some come to live there.

It's often noted—it's hard to miss—that at the edges of my realm, I've raised very high, very sharp towers. At the top of each burns a flame which cannot be extinguished. These towers are not extraordinarily practical as architectural objects. But I find them most useful. Each is a message to myself, like a note you might place on your own pillow. They're a defiance. They're visual mnemonics, and they're both simple enough, and strangely vast enough that, no matter how often I see them, they always make me pause and smile.

It's not a complex metaphor, nor an obscure one. That's not what I wanted. Simply put: they remind me of the unquenchable fire inside. The world will try to dowse that combustion in anyone; it's the nature of material reality to weigh heavily on the body, and for the brain to trick itself into believing that the body's complaints are complaints of the spirit. They are little acts of rebellion because each stands, as noted, a bit beyond my own territories. It means, technically, some poor fools can try to extinguish them. And I've been careful not to make it impossible; just very difficult. Those who painstakingly climb the towers to put out the flames become, at worst, frustrated, and at best, they're scorched.

(I see no need for subtlety in my metaphors. If I wanted subtle, I wouldn't live in a vast keep and give myself a flashy name. Standing out makes you a target; but sometimes you know you're doing your job if you have to dodge Fae-poisoned arrows.)

Oddly enough, I don't hate the people who take it upon themselves to scale my edifices. In fact, I rather like those who are burnt through determination and not sheer stupidity. Perhaps I am extending too much hope to believe they share a little kinship with me. But perhaps not. The more badly you are blistered, the more badly you are scarred. The more you are scarred, the more others know fear, because they see your scalding and associate it with their own vulnerability to injury and death. They see it as disfigurement. And you can tell a lot about people by how they treat those who are, like me, ugly.

I find that those newly seen as un-beautiful tend to turn, to change in their attitudes towards me. I still don't rejoice when it happens, though; I've been an outcast, and I wouldn't easily wish it on others. (It would be a little like caging people in order to shout speeches at them; outside of ethical questions, I want my bar set a little higher than "what will satisfy an audience which is literally captive". It leads to deep mental weakness when you play to a crowd which must laugh at your jokes or else perish on the spears of your guards. And a weak mind is no friend to the spellmaker.)

I mention it often, because I live by it: All magic has its price. Magic is not limitless, any more than any other thing with which we can interact directly. Not even the Gods have enough *mana* to inflict their every whim on this world. (For that matter, the fact that there *are* so many Gods, with so many opposing stories, is peculiar. This is a world of magic; the Gods have walked the Earth within the sight of reasonably reliable witnesses. They've wrought ridiculous changes which couldn't come from nature. And yet, we're not sure which Gods actually rule what. This suggests that the Gods themselves are quite limited. In fact, in what communion

I have with the Gods, I have often wondered if they are happy. I have often wondered if immortality suits them. As someone who committed a terrible act of necromancy, one night very long ago, with a very deceased God, I sometimes wonder if it is the dead Gods who got the best of the cosmic deal. But that's another tale.)

Say it, repeat it, tattoo it on the inside of your skin: *All magic costs.* It is the first thing you learn in my vocation; or at least, it should be. It is a principle to be found everywhere. But the simplest piece is that once you know magic exists, it's real, you can work with it yourself—then you have two basic choices. You either abandon it for reasons of morality, or difficulty, or lack of courage--or take it up, knowing that having a reach beyond that of an ordinary mortal means entirely new dangers hitherto unseen. You begin to realize that, though magic is constrained, it is also *vast.* You can do many things that are otherwise impossible; most of them will probably kill you, and many of them would ultimately be terribly fragile, but you *can* do them. You could walk to the Moon, with enough preparation; oh, it's more likely that, at some point, you'd lose concentration or energy or get a rune wrong and fall into space. But it's not *impossible.*

And every magical act is an experiment unto itself. It's thaumaturgy, not cooking. You can bake the same recipe a hundred times, and your stove might eventually give out, but if you duplicate the recipe, you'll duplicate the results. Not so with magic. Magic has a certain amount of sentience. Sometimes it gets bored. Sometimes, there is some unknown factor, some ambient remnant of sorcery lying around. Sometimes it acts through its favorite agent, coincidence. You trip or you stumble or you use a wrong component, and the spell mutates. Coincidence is how magic replicates itself under the very eyes of those who would most disbelieve it.

So any spell you cast could harm you. Any really powerful spell could *destroy* you. The same is true of technology, as is well-known. The same is really true of any extraordinary power. Magic differs from the others, not in raw *force,* but because it ultimately answers, not precisely to any set of laws or rules, but to itself alone. Aye, if you speak to the right Names in the right places, you'll likely achieve something like what you desire. But Names change—as I know better than anyone. Magic is unique in that it need *not* follow an ordinary logical or natural progression. It can be self-contradictory. It can warp without any reason or need. It can affect its own nature. Like me, magic defies destiny and defies preordination; and thus, any magic worth doing is magic which could do hurt you real bad. Any sufficiently powerful magic could destroy you in a manner more total and painful than you've ever imagined. If you're not prepared to take that risk, you ought to leave the supernatural altogether aside.

Why do you think the White Wizard casts so few spells?

If you took all sorcery from the equation, if we lived in a world without it, the White Wizard's psychological state would display what's going on, in the same way that a drop in sanguinary glucose leaves you exhausted. Even without thaumaturgical assistance, the natural chemicals of the body modulate in response to stimulus. That's relatively obvious. When people are throwing their love and adulation at you in mass quantities, though, it's mind-altering in ways you can't easily imagine unless you've experienced it, and it happens on a level that isn't even available to our cognizance.

It is scent and pheromones. It is in the way our language centers respond to tone of voice and subtle cues, the way our psyche responds to the perceptions of others. The White Wizard is covered in a glory vastly more *physical* than most people imagine. *Without* magic, it makes him powerful and *with* it, with the unconscious witch-energy of thousands of devoted believers, there is hypnotic command in his smallest words and there is psychic authority in an act as simple as walking across a room. He has all that power pouring into him, and it is glorious and it is delicious. I knew such things once, had them for my own. I possessed them for reasons that I now reject. The White Wizard has never considered declining that adulation, has never seen it as anything less than his due, has never seen himself as anything other than doing the greatest of works. That certainty is like a beam of deeply concentrated light, intense enough to carve through solid stone.

But the White Wizard does not cast many spells.

Spells are difficult, spells are tricky, and spells could go awry. He lives on the exaltation of others, but he does so to feed his ego alone; it's his actual propulsion. For him, it's a substitute for the will which is so necessary to enact magecraft. It's an incredible feeling, as I know well, but to experience it in full, you need to have an unquestioning certainty. I can't do that. I've *much* uncertainty. I question quite a lot. I am not sure about the world. I don't believe that I know the truth of every cause. I don't believe that everything I do is right; I don't even believe it's all right for *me* or true to myself, much less universally true. You can make mistakes about those things, confuse what you want to be, or what you might become, with what you currently are. The Wizard is *certain* he knows what is about to happen; I'm not even sure I've made the right *guesses*.

I think he leads a happier life than I do. But a more rewarding one? We'll see about that soon enough.

# Why Goblins Hide

Orcs live in caves. Goblins live in shadows. It's the pain of distance versus the pain of proximity.

Humans know the world as being full of creatures of darkness, a place simply pumped to *bursting* with all manner of Things in umbral spaces, things which *hate* them. Humans don't seem to have given much thought about who hated whom first.

(That's odd, actually. You'd figure it would be extraordinarily relevant. If you're going to have reason to jump at shadows, oughtn't you wonder precisely what you've done to make your dark reflection pissed off?)

(Then again, while curiosity is essential for the growth of society, it also fuels that pesky discontentment thing. And discontentment either gets channeled into appropriate paths and used by said society, or it gets you kicked right on out. Or—this option's my favorite—they use your ideas, and *then* they send you away.

Joke's on them, though. I will *always* have more ideas. They will *seldom* find someone like me.)

All right. As an exile, as former person of the day, I am insatiably curious: Why do the things of the Underdark hate those who dwell in sunlight?

I've given it much thought. Consider:

As far as we can tell, human culture evolved along what appears to have been some logical paths. Early *homo sapiens* needed shelter, and sometime early on, they started using that which was already around—namely, caves. (They certainly left enough crude drawings therein.)

(And the new inhabitants of those places, oddly enough, seldom choose to erase those leavings or blot them out. But they *do* respond. It's not unusual to discover a crude human cave painting next to an extremely intricate Goblin poem. Because taking the piss at others appears to be a nigh-universal trait.)

Cast your thoughts backwards. If humans are at a stage where they live in caves, they must be at a very early point in their development indeed. Perhaps they don't even have the resources to actually penetrate to the back of the caves with their vision, even at high noon. Perhaps they moved in simply with the *hope* that there was nothing inside... or the fear of something worse outside. Have you ever awakened at night with unknown breath on your head, coming from a place you can't see? Likely not, and yet, it's part of our programmed and collective memories. It does not endear to us those strange things who live in the inky places. We don't know how long humans dwelt in claustrophobic stone, but they surely got out as soon as they were capable.

Now look on the present, and consider the non-human sentients of this world. Ask yourself: *Why do they live in the dark?*

Is that how their eyes were naturally adopted? Is this a universe where certain things are built or made, not only nocturnal in a literal sense but somehow full of the stuff of night itself, and already in thrall to the forces of darkness? Are they part of the reason we have so many metaphors of shadow and ignorance, and why, when the fear of the gloom comes upon us, it's usually accompanied by a visceral hatred?

There's no way to really know the origin of something that bone-deep, but we *can* look at what we know of humans and make some inferences. Prayer-senders, wound-healers, toolmakers and weapon-builders all at once, incredibly aggressive and capable of deep calm and quiet, humans are insanely adaptable, both in mind and in body.

This last can be seen in the life arc of any human who has lived through interesting times, but it can also be viewed by just looking at some of our physical capabilities.

A human can run down a horse over time because horses, while more fleet of foot, do not have human fortitude, and they do not think well. They will run themselves to exhaustion, without stopping to get enough sustenance or rest--while humans will stalk them with patient endurance, cold-bloodedly eating and drinking and sleeping until the prey drops dead. (And even a stupid human, without much sustenance, eventually tracks down the horse; few can beat humans for sheer bloody-mindedness.)

What was our prehistory really like? Why do we assume it was very different from our current history?

Or, more to the point: Why did humans flee *from* caves, while Goblins fled *towards* them?

Again, consider:

What would happen if Goblins set up a camp near a human village tomorrow?

They could choose to co-exist happily, of course, enjoying the sun together. (Though this would probably come at a time of climate change, since it wouldn't happen until the ecosystem of Hell is reduced to sub-zero temperatures.)

The human village *might* flee. But unless it was an extremely isolated village, they would be far more likely run for some form of human authority, and the human authority would send organized, armed, armored forces to eradicate the Goblins. Every. damn. last. one.

What sort of defense would the humans have of this xenocidal impulse? That Goblins are ugly? That Goblins do not like humans?

Narratives matter. It *matters* whether Goblins have always slain humans on sight, thus making it necessary for humans to defend themselves—or if humans have always looked at Goblins, blinked in disgust, and reached for weapons, while the Goblins were still trying to fit their canines around a polite "Hello" in Human tongue.)

On the one side, we have the weight of human history, painstakingly recording the villainy of Goblins.

On the other side, we know that Goblins have lived in peace with the many races of the Underdark. That's a simple, provable fact.

We're led to two conclusions:

1. Narratives can lie, and they can lie big, as long as

2. Humans are happy to ignore what they can observe, in favor of a story which fits comfortably in their heads

.What do the Goblins say about this? The Goblins say very little. They're a quiet species. Not physically weak, nor physically unimpressive. They assuredly hunt for their dinners. They have long steely scimitar nails, predatory teeth, and even tusks. That's unusual for a humanoid species, because very large teeth get in the way of conversation, and very sharp claws get in the way of manual dexterity. It's peculiar to find both opposable thumbs and sentient behavior alongside some of nature's finest built-in killing tools, but it happened here.

Yet Goblins live in the dark places rejected by Orcs, and will flee even from the lowest things in the underdark. Goblins cower although they are not cowardly.

Why?

Goblins tell a certain tale, and as the great battle approaches on the horizon, that tale becomes of interest. (Well, it is of interest to *me*. Of course, nothing the Goblin does ought to interest Mankind in general, because there is nothing but evil and foulness to be gained otherwise. Everyone knows that. Even considering otherwise would make you suspect, and that would not be good. A Goblin-sympathizer in your midst? Report him at once!)

But their constraints are not mine. So let me speak of a thing:

*The tale of the Goblins is built every single night.*

As Goblins go to sleep, in the comforting hour or so before dawn (for Goblins end their days when humans would begin their own) – each tribe gathers to speak some of the story. It is never spoken all at once; that would not be possible. If a hundred goblins, each of whom knew a lifetime of the story, could spend a lifetime telling it to you, they could not pass on even a meaningful fraction of the ideas within, much less the real substance. The tale is a living thing; it is made by many different Goblins in many different ways, and their children and those of their clan, pass it on in pieces. And through a process no one outside their race has ever been permitted to understand, they decide which pieces remain in the song cycle and which are gone, and in some manner which is not mystical and is, to me, all the more awe-inspiring therefore, the pieces of the tales they tell inform us and make meaning.

(Then again—you should never underestimate the power of the stories which survive systematic attempts to destroy them.)

My own theory is that, though the actual yarn is much too long to tell, the fact that it is sung every night, and includes the most mundane things alongside the most heroic, makes it the kind of tale which endures. Hearing a piece of it, you might find out, in some detail, about how some tribe survived a great famine of a thousand years before; or you might find out the unbelievably ordinary, yet lovingly described, dental habits of someone named "Zog" who lived before humans had books.

I like the story of Zog. He really understood flossing.

He was not significant; he did not do significant things; and yet he is honored, because *none need be insignificant.*

Now that, *that* is a heritage.

Picking out a part is like pulling a piece off a leaf and trying to use it to describe the tree which bore it. But there are some pieces which appeal more to humans than others. Here's a bit I translated, is about one of the most frequent themes in the Goblin world: The Sun.

*Sunlight could be compared.*

*To the ripest of fruits, or, if you could find bees whose abilities might please the mouth of Gods, you might compare it to honey. You might compare it to the finding of water in the deepest underground when you had been lost and you otherwise would shortly die of thirst.*

*But most of all,*

*Sunlight is best compared to sunlight.*

*And it is the thing we shun. We understand greed, and do not always consider it immoral. How could any being or species advance without feeling the most urgent of desires?*

*They could not.*

*If you covet something possessed by another, perhaps you might share that thing. Perhaps you might trade for that thing. And perhaps you might take that thing.*

*If you take it away from another, perhaps you will feel shame. And that is a birth of anger, because anger drowns shame, and shame is a reminder that you owe something to another.*

*It is a weakness, in a thief. This is why we rouse the anger of Men: for they cannot let themselves be chastened by what they have done. They say we take the children of men when we can, **and we do**. They say we drink the blood of men when we can, **and we do**. They say we set fire to the works of men when we can, **and we do**.*

*What they do not say is what we once **gave** to men.*

*We do not speak of it ourselves because if we named it, we would not be able to bear the loss. And also because, by now, we do not remember. Not any one of us. We have knowingly erased the thought, because we used to be blinded by rage and grief, and that is not good. Not if you wish to live long enough to see revenge. We gave humans a thing they wanted, a long time ago, when they had less than a handful of words.*

*And they accepted it. And they kept it. And they named it. And once they named it, they took it for their own. And they most certainly forgot that it had ever been anything else.*

*And now, it is theirs.*

We tried to trade for daylight, long ago. We were repaid with a testing of our ability to go to war, and the question of whether our race united could destroy their race united; and we retreated. Perhaps in cowardice. Perhaps for survival. Perhaps because, while we want to live, we do not desire life--no one desires life, really, or desires anything in the world, for that matter--so much as the humans desire to own **every single piece of sunlight everywhere**.

So it is theirs today, and we tell other stories.

For now.

For now.

For now.

   For now.

# PART III: ENTROPY WAXES FAT

## DIARY OF THE CHOSEN ONE: ESCAPE FROM THE ORCISH CAVES

Do you know what a dead Orc looks like?

Despair.

I'm perfectly happy to be rescued. And I'd certainly choose their deaths over mine.

But why did they have to sing before they moved to take my life? Was it some kind of ritual?

I don't think so. I think perhaps I ought not have let them know I speak Orc.

I suppose I wouldn't be alive if I hadn't done so. Although—at least being dead would mean my mind was at rest, not infested with these circling, scratching thoughts.

They didn't even take my notebook. They treated it as if it was a part of my body. They not only fed me, they fed it—they brought me quills and ink.

Was I to leave another journal for another Chosen One? Is this a part of our pattern? Do we all end up writing missives—to ourselves, to the thoughts in the back of our heads? ....how many before me were the sort of people who would write down their current lives, with the idea that someone who replaced us, someone who came after we were gone, might seek some of the same answers, and we could help?

How many dead Chosen Ones? How many notebooks? Where does it end?

Why am I humming inhuman melodies from my captivity?

There is an odd sense to Orcish music. Humans often like neatly rhymed couplets and melodies which repeat, to reinforce meaning. Orcs seem only to sing communally. Their voices walk a twisty line between harmony and dissonance. They do not rhyme—not in their mother tongue, and translating their work into rhyme makes it seem like nursery talk. They speak very directly—the way humans do, before we teach ourselves that it's impolite.

Orcs have a rich and vast oral tradition. They have to. We burned all their books.

This is what they sang me, as near as I can translate it:

Little mother of the death of our sons,
Little blade, opener of small and vital veins
Tiny movement of rocks which caves in the home,
We almost want to let you kill us
For we are tired.
Tired of raising our children to hate you.
They were scholars once, and now, warriors all,
They give that blood that it may seep through cracks
And find its way to the surface world.
Killing us is your destiny.
Killing you is no pleasure.
We could pile human bodies a thousand high,
Stand atop them,
Drink in the sun,
And still not lose the cold
Of living in the dark.
Kill us,
Or die for us.
We want you to end our pain, and we want our children to live in the light.
We cannot have both.
You come,
And the next comes,
And the next comes,
And we try to stay brave.
We taste the sun—just long enough for you to pull it away.
And so we kill you—before we lose our resolve,
Your body instead our ours.

Orcs are savage and ferocious, but they sang, and they spent forever sharpening their knives, as if they half-knew that, given a bit of time, my rescue would come. They did not last long when it did.

A horde of Orc-kind, too many to count, boiled up from some deep place just as we reached the cave mouth. They did nothing. They just watched us as we left.

I could read it in their eyes: something stayed their hands this time, but when next we saw them, they would be implacable, merciless, furious, unnaturally, monstrously savage.

Because they are desperate.

They know that the end of the Dark Lord is the end of their dream of rebirth. Human settlement will be safe, and the sun will not shine on ugly, monstrous, misshapen forces.

I am their death. They know it. Now I know it, too.

# Does Everybody Really Want To Rule The World?

I toppled the One True King to be here. I ended a long line of monarchs. Histories tell us they were just and noble and good.

But that doesn't seem much like the humanity I know. And I'm certain they were human—I've tasted the blood.

Have you studied much in the way of human history? You ought, if you plan to be active in its affairs. A suggestion: seek out the stories which most conflict with what you want to believe.

They may or may not be lies. But the ability to listen to those who disagree, even if you're going to fight them with everything you have, is a strength; the inability to do so is a fatal weakness.

It's hard to have a good sense of what went on before. It's difficult to capture a living moment in words at the best of times, and more challenging still to try to know what happened in the midst of chaos. Still, from my studies, as far as I can tell, the best model for governance is to be part of a fairytale kingdom, with a wise and just ruler, in an upbeat children's story. Preferably one with lots of pictures.

The problems likely start with genetics: It turns out that Royals are not, in fact, born to rule. Or, at least, they're not born to rule *well*, which is pretty much the rub.

And sadly, fairytale kingdoms work *poorly*. It's not just that they're fairytales and thus not terribly real; we've seen stranger and more mythical attempts at leadership in our time. The problem is that Fairytales attract Good Faeries, and thus Bad Faeries; Evil Queens; Huntsmen, and, of course, The Grand Vizier. And all of those tend to lead to ruination. Even in the aforementioned yarn, you need to hope that you're in a comparatively *modern* chronicle, where everything is required by the narrative to work out well. Because it's not terribly likely, otherwise, that's you'll have an ending that's particularly good for anyone who doesn't live in the nicer parts of the Palace. Which means that saying "They all lived happily ever after" ought to have a footnote, "Except for the many, many people who totally didn't."

Nobles and commoners share a common challenge: they'd like to benefit from the world. They have to; otherwise, evolution would select against them. If your base survival traits don't include "survive" (and try to thrive), you're pretty much going to do neither.

And thus the difficulty: one man's wine is another man's deadly neurotoxin. You need a hell of a surplus of resources to get to a point where "more for you" isn't "less for me". Not even magic produces something for nothing—quite the opposite, actually.

Assuming you could create, say, ten times the ordinary amount of crops and livestock usually available given a particular set of resources (how? You can't just wave a magic wand at the problem; trust me, I've got, like, eleven magic wands, and the likeliest resolution there is just that you electrocute yourself)—even if you could get all that extra stuff somehow, you still have to figure out how to divide it all up. What did it cost you to be able to have that kind of surplus, and how willing are you to share the fruits of your labor with those who didn't help?

It's a difficult problem, but fortunately, you can kick it upstairs to the Ruler of the Land.

Who is busy dealing with this, *and every other problem people couldn't solve.*

Assuming, of course, that said monarch isn't busy dealing with, oh, a revolution or a curse or (Gods help us all)--a plague of glitter o'er the land.

In other words:

It's all very well and good to want to topple "Evil"; but what, exactly, is the plan to replace it with some kind of better leadership, "Good" or otherwise?

# Diary of the Chosen One: Off to See the White Wizard

Hobbit-weed has always made the Wizard mellow. It's how he's frequently portrayed.

(It's an act. Isn't everything an act with him? Every move studied, every gesture practiced?

But isn't that what you actually need in order to effect change?

Most people do not really look more beautiful when they're furious or in tears, no matter what the sagas say. Human foibles and fallibilities are fuel for tragedy and comedy, but not for drama. If you want to be taken seriously, can you really be faulted for a desire to appease those around you? If what people want, if what they care about, if what they listen to is the act, the artifice, the crafted phrase instead of the stumbling reality, should he hobble himself by showing his actuality instead of his act?

I don't show the Wizard my true face; I oughtn't criticize him for failing to show me his.

I suppose the difference is, I don't know what my true face is. I think he set his a long time ago, and then hid it away.)

(Reality does not, in fact, seem more true than fiction. Well-made fiction, which is crafted to appeal to our minds, has every right to compete with reality, and win, doesn't it?)

If you could tear away every piece of pretense, your own eyes would deceive you. It's why are able to look at stick figures and see humans; our minds extrapolate the actuality from the symbols.

Still, some things matter more than others. An Orc feeding its young is not the same as an Orc with an Elvish arrow though its back.)

"I think you've been lying to me."

The Wizard doesn't even look up at me at my words. His smoke rings continue curling into the figures of strange creatures and runes. It's some of the only magic he does. Like many of his actions, it's strange, unmistakably sorcerous, and possibly one of the most useless things you could plausibly imagine.

"So the Dark has tainted you," he replies.

I just look at him.

Now he finally looks up at me. "And if it has?" I respond. I am suddenly aware that his staff is ironwood, and my skull is not that hard.

I think this is the first time he sees me, really notices my presence. I doubt that he knows my name, but I think he realizes it wasn't always "Chosen One". His eyes suddenly smolder—not with enchantment, but with an utterly unguarded intensity.

"Then you must burn it out. And quickly."

I don't say anything.

"Generations not born, not even conceived as ideas, will labor under a yoke of slavery, and all that will free them is us. Is our tiny band. All that will free them Is you."

Images tumble across my head; troubling thoughts of what is and is not slavery, questions of life under the Rightful King instead of the Dark Lord, treacherous thoughts which want to disagree. And yet—

Magic is real. The True Lineage exists. Even if the Wizard wrote the prophecy, he wrote it by being alive centuries before my grandparents existed. I haven't lived a lot of my one lifetime, much less the Wizard's generations of knowledge. What do I know?

And it's not as if I haven't been in communication with the Dark. Though I think that, in general, the Dark is as confused and messed-up as I am.

Now his voice is soft. "The Orcs would slay us all, you know. Just to stand here where you and I stand, to make the earth their foul place. Goblins prefer no flesh to human flesh. And the Dark Lord has no love for mankind." He pauses.

"I am ancient, and the gulf between myself and the shorter-lived is very wide. But you, you have it in your heart to speak true, and to do right. Someday, you will stand in an honored place beside the King. Someday, we will smoke pipes together, and speak of matters great and small, and we will remind the land of justice."

I don't know where I find any voice at all, but I do. "Like we reminded the Orcs?"

His gaze doesn't waver, not even for a moment. "Precisely as we reminded the malformed things; exactly as we taught them mercy."

"Mercy? In forcing them deep underground?"

His head returns to staring off into the distance. "Mercy that they live, child. Mercy that they live."

He turns away from me. I know that look. Nothing more will he speak tonight.

# A Night Of Unsettling Dreams

Tonight – as on so many nights – the Chosen One and I mirror each other. (How do I *know* this? Mind-reading is not really possible; I've tried, but the brain is a swirling eruption of thoughts, images, and associations, sorted into order only by that peculiar, unique, and impenetrable thing we call "consciousness". I can get glimpses and fragments, but that's about it. The Chosen One must have let me in, at some point. And I must have let her in. What a stupid thing to do on both sides! One of us needs to kill the other; why get emotionally close enough to make it wrenching?)

(And why do I have to share her nightmares, of all things?)

She dreams:

(She dreams of death and flame, and I dream the same. And between us two, who dreams of what? Whose mind is inflicting this on us?)

Forgive me; I am drunk. Alcohol kills the dreams a bit, or at least, it lulls my gears temporarily to quiet, allowing me, in turn, to sleep with relative peace. Though the drowse is always thin. I spent a long time breaking down the barriers between dream and reality, hoping to raise the cryptocrystalline things of my inner vision, and little did I realize that, along with the spiraling revelatory joys of vision made into life, I also brought forth that and those who would see all my works fall. Create a thing which inspires awe, and expose it to enough humans, and there will eventually be at least one who says, not only, "I wish I had made that," but, "If I *remove* the one who made that, I can give that thing my *own* name".

Humans are humans. All of us have memories which are made of smudges on a fallible meat canvas, and we can't admit it; we can't be honest and say that our minds don't hold a perfect image of precisely what happened. So we turn our backs while the hindbrain quietly fills in lines and connects dots and makes an image which, when we look at it anew, we find pleasing. One who has laid a brick in a foundation is entitled to say, "I was a part of the making of that thing". One who has laid in a hundred bricks in a thousand might decide, "It was my bricks which truly caused this thing to be erected; it's *mine*."

You might think a Dark Lord would either be without an instant's doubt, or else be wracked with constant uncertainty about herself. Neither is the case. I made who and what I am through effort and will (and accident, and fortune both kind and unkind) – just like anyone who's ever built something of value. Sometimes I am dearly sure of that value; sometimes I doubt it beyond reckoning.

Sometimes, I doubt which bricks I laid, myself.

The Chosen One has constant nightmares. I don't blame her. She isn't simply nearing her death; she's nearing it in the company of those who, when they hear "Watch my back", mentally insert, "...for the optimal place to position a few daggers". And why not? Treachery follows power, and much as the Wizard claims to be an underdog, his power is writ large. He seems utterly certain that he'll win. There are few temptations sweeter than that of picking up the mantle of noble struggle, while being fairly sure that your opponent will go down.

There's a little darkness in the purest hearts. And a lot of darkness in the hearts which most loudly claim their purity.

It's much easier to live a life certain that you are in the right, and that the sunlight is yours by virtue of virtue, than to question yourself. The first lies you hear, when you believe yourself to be a hero, are most often from sent your heart to your head.

Not only is the world not black and white–but "black and white" doesn't have the meaning we tend to ascribe to it.

It's useful to say that light opposes darkness, but it isn't really true. As visual phenomena, the range of what can be seen depends, both on the optical apparatus of the viewer, and the types of illumination available. Ultraviolet is beyond the viewing spectrum of the human eye, but that doesn't abnegate its existence. If we can conceive a total darkness, some place where no eye could see, what would be the counterpoint? Even if you had a light of infinite brightness, it would simply blind the onlooker, and the result would be the same–you could not see.

As conceptual manifestations, ideas of light and dark are most meaningful when they explore the places in-between. I embrace darkness, but it's not an end, it's a means. It permits me to extend myself beyond the fragility of day, the ordinary waking pattern of our species. There's nothing wrong with the norms; it's just helpful to recognize that they both preserve and ensnare us.

I could feel guilty for adding a bit to the disquiet in the Chosen One's heart, but I don't. Surety is a narcotic which masks the fact that you're dying. Losing it is a gift.

The glare of Sunlight shows us so much of the world; but you can't see the pretty parts without seeing all the walls.

In Darkness, you might believe you could slip through the cracks of the world, and find hidden and more interesting places.

And you might not be wrong.

*The Day forbids; the Night beckons.*

# WAR

---

"When the battle's won and lost
Leave the fools to count the cost
And those alive will have discovered
It's with glory they are covered."
 -War Song of Man

Soon, the air will ring with the screams of Orcs and Men.

Personally, I'd rather have fiddle music, but, unsurprisingly, I was not asked for my opinion.

The White Wizard is in his element. He knows more tales of battle than I ever thought existed. They all conclude either in glorious triumph, or in heroism that resounds throughout the ages. This seems statistically unlikely to me. Why would Evil persist in going to war if Good kept smashing its head in on a consistent basis?

You'd think one or two historic battles would end with an inventory of lost farms and artisans, and some very hungry winters. Oddly, it seems nobody talked much about that.

The Wizard has assured me that we will win because Right is on our side. I sort-of want to want to ask him, if that is the thing that really counts, why he didn't have this battle a few generations ago.

But he's been paying less attention to me, and I'm pretty happy with it staying that way. He keeps telling me that I shall learn many valuable lessons on my journey, but the last time he caught me with his spellbooks, he screamed, "FOOL OF A ROOK!", or something equally incoherent. I really thought the guy would burst a blood vessel or something. Anyway, I keep mostly to myself.

This would be a grand time for the Wizard to make some great working of spellcraft, to give us some advantage over the foe. That's clearly not happening. Either he really prefers just running his mouth, or he is considerably lacking in mystical prowess.

(I asked him about this. "It is wrong for me to meddle too much in human affairs," he said. "They must choose their own destiny."

"Bleedin' hell, you mean, like the way you pulled me out of my cottage and threw me on the back of a horse?"

"Your destiny is special, for you are Chosen."

"...and what about those poor bastards over there. What were they chosen for—premature graves?"

The Wizard laid a comforting hand on my shoulder. "The stresses of this time take their toll on us all. Worry not. I take no anger at your rash words, because I know the strain you undergo."

I narrowly resisted biting him.)

What's it all add up to?

Hm. Methinks the Wizard is a bit small in the magical department. Do you suppose that accounts for the absolutely massive staff he insists on carrying about everywhere?

Just speculation, you understand.

The lack of sorcerous backup is particularly noticeable right now, because even at this remove from The Dark Lord's hold, we can see peculiar things—unnatural colors in the sky, shafts of heavy lightning, and once, on an especially disturbing night, the brief but total disappearance of the Moon. The White Wizard explained this as "an eclipse", but we've seen those before, and they aren't normally accompanied by a shimmery BOOM—as if the harmonies of things celestial were rapidly brought into a disturbing crescendo we had never previously been able to hear. Or something big blew up, whichever.

I don't know that we can win this one.

The armies of Men and Elves seem extremely optimistic—arrogant, really. The armies of the Dwarves appear unusually taciturn. They aren't even drinking much. They keep glancing upwards, as if something's wrong with the daylight.

They stopped singing about gold and started to sing about mining disasters.

It's actually an improvement.

# THE GREAT BATTLE APPROACHES

There is nothing like fighting an epic battle against countless mighty foes to make you *really* question your line of work.

As I consider the multitudes arrayed before me, with mighty swords and spears and axes and crossbows, I cannot help but think: "Bugger this for a lark."

In general, I believe there are two kinds of warriors: those who do not fear death because they are deeply enlightened, and those who do not fear it because they are deeply stupid.

I don't want to die. And I'm not ashamed of it. There are things I want to do first.

Oh, granted, death is not the end. The end is when they make your name into a mockery and a lie. The end is when they tell themselves what they are, they tell you what you are, and it *sticks*. That is the true death, and that is why the big winners of any great battle are the eaters of carrion—literal and metaphorical.

They'll try to do this while you live, but it's often much more convenient to malign your corpse.

(Though I can tell you from experience—there's nothing quite like that moment when they think they're safely insulting your cold body, and you rise back up, bloodstained dagger in one hand, wand in the other. As I mentioned—not immortal, just harder to kill than people apparently expect.)

I *still* don't want it all to end. Which is part of why I now have an army between my body and my enemies.

It's not that I've no thirst for the coming battle. But I despise the waste.

I imagine—no, at this point, I know—that the Chosen One questions why my army spends its time within my realm, as opposed to out in conquest.

Sure, war is useful if simple harm is your goal. But it's not often an efficient solution. I'm not one to wax poetic on the glories of battle in the first place, but any politician knows: facing an opponent straight on is a paltry thing compared to either making better policy, or sticking a dozen knives into a dozen carefully-selected backs...depending on your motivations for seeking power in the first place. Indeed, this is why politicians generally stay behind when called to battle. Because they are "too valuable" to fight, because they're often too old, and because they have no taste for the uneconomical situation of trying to slay a hundred nonentities, when they could, through words and backstage actions, devour the reputation and the power of one equal, and thus become greater. Why *not* send legions into battle, if you know there's no risk to your own skin, and you stand to look shiny?

I don't have "equals" to devour, and the distraction of combat is not of use to magical result.

Also, unlike my opponents, I recognize: All war is risk. All battles have cost (because, always, always, all things have a cost. Magic's prices can be subtler, crueler, more unexpected, because magic sometimes gets to pick what it wants. But *every* opportunity taken, mundane or metaphysical, is a path opened at the expense of every move *not* made.)

Nothing's free; in fact, the costliest thing of all is the overconfidence of believing that what happens next will be *easy*.

*Toxic certainty is the whispering voice that tells you that you cannot lose. It's in your head while you sleep. And it's a forerunner of what comes next--the other whispering voice that wakes you, to let you know you're already dead.*

# About That Shining Army Of Light

Vast is the army of humans, coming cloaked in their armor of righteousness. You might not be able to see it, because that armor is invisible. All right, in fact, it's nonexistent. Or more specifically, it exists, but only in their minds. That's also why "righteousness" can take this form. Because how else would virtue appear in the shape of a wholesale desire for slaughter?

And indeed, "righteousness" comes as burning veins and fury and shouts and bellows and a hundred thousand sword thrusts, each one delivered in the belief that it gets the attacker a bit closer to sainthood.

If humans devoted this much energy to tasks which did *not* involve the death throes of those whose faces they dislike, their societies would might be a little improved.

Does humanity unite just to make war against things which are simply displeasing to their eyes? Certainly not. Everything they fight just *happens* to be ugly, but the horrible truth is, the dread Foes are all outrought *immoral*; ask anyone and the'll tell you it's so. (Well, ask anyone *but* the ones you're fighting; as previously noted, it's horribly immoral to speak to those who are known to be immoral...)

You may not understand just how sanctified these combats are. Trust me, every battle is conveniently one upon which the Gods have smiled a white-toothed approval, a big goofy grin of "Go out there and stab 'em in the kidneys; this is just what we want!" No-one's heard any Gods actually talking, but the priests on their payroll assure them that this is what's happening; why else would they be on the payroll?

I'm so weary.

The humans have come, ostensibly, for me. But in fact, they have arrived because their glands spout eruptions of pleasure when they get a chance to combine adrenaline and moral certainty. Though humans are very intelligent, there is little intellect prefers more than surfing a wave of delirious passion, brewed by their most aggressive neurochemical glanding, while the piece which calls itself "consciousness" wildly flits around in search of rationalizations. Remember, it's not about the high, it's about the more fiber of the attacker. That's why there've been so many totally, utterly just wars. And we've got the trampled crops to prove it--a sure sign of success.

They come for me, they come for us, and most of all, they come for their own enjoyment.

I plan to spoil their day. In fact, I plan to spin it thoroughly out of the sunshine and straight into the Abyss.

# The Joys Of Ignorance

While we're on the subject of ignorance, it's also common knowledge that Trolls don't have a culture. Neither do Goblins. Neither do Dragons.

It's false knowledge, but common nonetheless.

Why not? Things which build meaningful lives might be "human", and humans only give that status to the beautiful, like their good friends the Elves. (Fun fact: The most common Elvish word for human can be translated fairly directly as "Troll snack". The White Wizard tends to translate that word as "Brothers". I'm not sure if he's that ignorant, or if he's in on the joke.)

(Have you ever been to an Elven banquet? They put upon each table both wine and poison. And drink a little of both. Because they believe the latter makes them stronger? No, because the taste feels right in their mouths.)

*Human* culture is a thing riddled with the most fascinating pieces of opinion, and the most extraordinary sets of implausibly-fitted ideas. But don't worry: it all finally comes together to build a narrative that makes a preponderance of no sense at all, when you think about it.

....maybe you should, in fact, worry about that.

I can't say that I blame Humans for all this. To be fair, nobody likes hearing unpleasant things about themselves, and people tend to expect you to try to put yourself in the best possible light. So if you're the sort of monarch who doesn't censor the histories, you're admirable; you should also expect to appear worse, in the official histories, than *all* the monarchs who have standing orders to put to death anyone who sees their bad hair days. We barely write down what our leaders do with any accuracy, unless forced. How much less, then, do we write down the actions of the Orcs, the Trolls, the things of the Underdark, except to paint them, broadly, in literal and metaphorical blood?

This might be a problem, of course, if one wants to get an accurate idea of their capabilities. But that's okay—blot out their names often enough, and they'll just go away, right?

War's a good time to dust off the history books, since most sentient species just love to talk about battles, but, aside from the fairly small number which are written by those who actually fought, the process is frustrating. It's damn hard to find a decent historical account in an essentially imaginary kingdom.

Though reading between the lines, watching dynasties rise and fall, you start to recognize a constant: once you've a monarchy which whose lineage was "born to rule, by the will of the Gods", it is an easy theological step to recognize that if the king don't like something, it's gotta be Evil.

And everyone knows the cure for Evil is fire.

# Diary of the Chosen One: Strangers I Have Been

People like to think that somewhere—perhaps in the chest area, maybe as some kind of centerline organ near the heart—is something called the "self". It is made up of their experiences, and who and what they are. This is a comforting illusion; but 'self' has no anatomical home. It's too much a product of things other than the mind, and it changes far too often to be pinned down.

I've spent much too much time wondering not just "What am I?" and "Where am I?", but also "Where is the part of me that knows who the hell I am?"

How strange this journey's been, meeting and being the center of attention of hundreds of people. I've learned more about humans, much faster, than I ever would have if I'd stayed in my village, or indeed, lead any life I'd ever imagined.

And how likewise weird that it was my original village, itself, which taught me one of the more persistent lessons of this entire mess.

See, a very heartening piece of the journey, helping dispel some of my doubts and concerns, has been the sheer number of people who've had horrible, personal experiences with the Dark Lord. Some of those experiences are vastly too hideous to recount; certainly I have no conscious desire to think about them, much less give them strength by writing them down. Suffice to say that the Dark One seems to have spent much time inflicting individual miseries.

Though it eventually the math got weird. So many claimed to have been personally affected by the Dark Lord, or to have seen unspeakable horrors fall upon "a close friend". The Night Tyrant must spend a vast amount of of time among the people, wreaking individual harm; perhaps that makes sense, if all that creature does is seek out individual pain, like a sadistic predator playing with helpless prey. But how the hell does the Dark Lord ever get anything ELSE done?

Putting that aside, it gave me hope for the morality of my quest to find that the creature must be one of luminescent foulness, for each person said, "Of course, I always knew there was nothing but evil within that body. You could tell. Long before this person became Dark Lord, I could see there was something deeply awry, but I told none, for I was afraid." Extraordinary for the despot to have risen so high when it was, apparently, visible for all the world to see that the creature was a monster. I have dutifully put this in my notes.

It strikes me as strange that the land has seen so many of the Dark Lord's individual horrors; wherever does one get the downtime to do so much, and walk among the people inflicting one-on-one atrocities?

It became less strange, and a bit more disturbing, when, in the course of our travels, we passed through my own village. Well, "mine" in the sense of it being where I was born and raised. It's not as if I had any real roots in that place, or they were sorry to see me go, or that I'd had any friends..

Or so I thought. But I was wrong. It turns out, once we arrived, that everyone called me by my first name. (And many of them mispronounced it.) And I began to hear them speak of me.

**I was so beloved. They had always known I was destined for great things. I was the close friend of, yes, each and every one of the denizens of my place of birth.**

I was approached by more than one of the people who had been my bullies, my tormentors, my harsh and seemingly arbitrary judges. The first time it happened, it was with someone of whom my memories were particularly unfond. I prepared for a fight—now that I knew how to do so, my persecutor was, should she start anything, about to get wrecked.

She shocked me by smothering me with hugs and kisses. She spoke loudly about the many fun times we'd had together. Glancing over her shoulder during one of her hard-to-dodge embraces, I looked at her left hand. Yes; there was still a very large scar. This was exactly who I thought it was. That scar was from the day she and some others had decided to see if I was human, or some kind of ugly amphibian, something that could breathe underwater. They'd done it by—eventually—overpowering me and holding me facedown in a cistern. For the first ten seconds, I was angry and scared. Thirty seconds in, I began to think: even if they don't intend to do it, they're going to drown me. And either they're too stupid to realize, or they just don't care.

*That's when I stopped flailing my arms, and grabbed her hand with both of mine. I wrenched my head around and brought my teeth down on her hand. I bit with every intention of severing tendon and bone; either they were going to let me breathe, or the price she'd pay for my death would be never using that goddamn hand for anything else, ever again.*

*She let me up; more specifically, she eventually let go, screaming, waving her bleeding appendage, and before they could decide what to do, I ran.*

*As she was going on and on about how much she and I had always been close, I just kept staring at the toothmarks, carved through her skin. They would never heal. When I finally pushed myself away, I heartily agreed about our lifelong friendship, and told her that I hoped she was well, and happy, and that the Dark Lord had not crossed her path.*

*How long did it take her to "remember" some ill done to her by the Dark Lord? I forget what it was. But her friends agreed with her, adding stories of their own. They were pretty good stories. Almost as compelling as the stories of the longtime rapport between myself and then.*

*It's odd. For my own part, the closest I come to remembering a "rapport" is that they taught me how to swear by showering abuse on my head.*

*Did they believe anything they were saying? Had they simply forgotten what they were to me, and I to them? I think they did, at least some of them; I don't think all of them were lying. Especially since it's strange to lie about me, to me. Unless you've made yourself believe something hard enough that you now think it's real.*

*Who doesn't want to say they've been personally hurt by the Dark Lord? They're not nice people, but they don't have to be liars; all you need to do is see the Dark Lord hurrying through your village, even on a broomstick, and add an ounce of something important—a mumbled incantation, a secret sign—and then your head connects it, clearly, easily, with some illness you suffered, some setback in business or love, some fear you had then which persists to this day.*

*And who, in the village of the Chosen One, will say that they didn't always love me? I hear they're planning a statue in the village* square. I imagine they'll treat it with far more respect than they showed me, when I lived here.

Have I mentioned that I do not sleep often, or well?

# ON THE MAJESTY OF ELVES

At this time, I'd like to reiterate something seldom perceived by even the most scholarly non-native speakers of Elvish: *It's composed almost entirely of sarcasm.*

There are a number of reasons this goes unnoticed. For one thing, Elvish is a most difficult tongue, and it requires enormous toil to gather even the most rudimentary understanding. Secondly, almost no-one undertakes that task unless they are mortally in love with that shiny, sparkly race.

And the third note is, perhaps, a corollary of the first: the few who've learnt the language and *aren't* spellbound by the glamour of Elves are those very, very few who have fallen from grace.

And we are, after all, villains. Everyone says so. Who'd believe a monster over a graceful and magical ally of humankind?

Nonetheless, you might find it strange that nobody's picked up on an entire parlance that is effectively a structure for conveying hatefulness. But there are further reasons why this might be. For example, even to a fluent speaker, the words of Elves are esoteric, cryptic, and convey peculiar meanings, which might not entirely follow human conceptions of truth or logic.

Most importantly, the sarcasm is not at *all* nuanced. It is not, as with human speech, irony contrasted in context with straight talk. Elves never speak directly, not even among themselves. For humans, "my friend" might indicate an ally or companion, or it might sardonically refer to an enemy. For elves, it always, always means "enemy" or "mark" or sometimes "plaything".

It's not that Elves are never sincere; but even their sincerity, their love, their passions have little knives. An Elf who says "I will love you forever" means "I will love you forever, or until I grow tired of you, whichever comes first". Short are the attention spans of the Elves, though very long indeed will they foster a grudge.

(I have been known to hold a grudge for an aeon or two, myself.)

Elves delight in suffering. They love the pain of foes, but so, too, do they feast on the sorrow of friends. For Elves hold one secret very dear: they do not truly think of *anyone* as friends, themselves included. Some are sociopathic, and have never chosen to learn the skill of cultivating a little empathy (because it is essential that everyone be replaceable, and a life of fungible contacts only feels hollow if you've ever felt connection). Some are empaths, never seeking understanding that they're now so intoxicated by hate and self-righteousness that they've lost other emotions.

For all that they look tall, Elves are among the smallest, meanest souls in Creation.

# DIARY OF THE CHOSEN ONE: SHITE MY COMPANIONS SAY

I wonder if my companions know that they repeat themselves a lot.

Not like someone who nags (though they surely do that as well). They do it like people who've never had an outside thought enter their heads.

I recognize the value of repeating a mantra of determination; I have my own. Simple ones. "I will not give up." "I will not let it end here." And also, "Punching your companions is unhelpful. Go into the forest and practice unarmed combat against a tree."

(My knuckles are a bit bloody, but they've grown stronger with time, as I was told they would. Close the fist tightly enough, and you can strike an increasingly durable substance with your bare hands. Which is quite preferable to the instinctive act of banging your head against the damn thing until the frustration goes away.)

Our Dwarven comrade keeps saying "The only way to the Light is to tunnel through the Dark." I like that. He does not, as some wags would believe, get drunk and sing about the joys of gold, exactly. He gets drunk and chants:

"Axe for Orc, axe for Man
Pick for Wolf, and miner's plan;
Dagger for the scheming Elf;
Tunnel cave-in for yourself."

I find his nihilism to be refreshing, when I'm surrounded by idiots. Though there's this line that he only says when he's very, very deep in his cups, or sometimes talking in his sleep:

"Deep in the mine, where dark takes hold;
Deep in the mind, no tales are told.
It ain't likely you'll live to get old
But dearly, dearly may your life be sold."

He's mentioned that he fights alongside us because the Dark Lord chooses to build cathedrals to strange Gods—about which he is uncaring—but he builds them out of gold, and that means less gold for him.

I feel like he's lying, but I don't know what he has to lie about.

I told him once, from within my own cups, that his actions looked greedy and selfish. He smiled and said, "We are the Dwarves; it is our destiny to bring shining things out of deep caverns, hold them up to the sun, then return them to our underground homes, to be looked at by only ourselves. Others call it greed for a simple reason: They want our gold, and they can't have it."

I said that Orcs also lived underground, and asked if he felt a kinship with them. He got a curious look on his face. Then he said a thing I would hear a thousand times:

"We should dig where Orcs must dwell.
They want the Deep? Send them to hell."

I dislike the Dwarf. I dislike him less than any other in my midst.

# YOU ARE WHAT YOU ARE EATEN BY

*As the actual battle approaches, the human world begins to speak of me more and more. Not that they ever forgot me, but for a time, they turned to other things. I don't have to seek it out to see it; it's in the background of every casual glimpse I catch as the Wizard and his company ride through various towns. I see more (worthless) protection sigils chalked on more homes, I feel more tension everywhere humans live, and—of course—I hear all manner of things I'm said to have done. It's deeply creative. As always, I wonder where I'd find the time to do so many personal wrongs. I am endlessly enthralled, and sometimes disgusted, to watch what fascinating new kinds of outrages one can commit if the only criteria for belief is "Someone said this happened". Seems like an odd way to spend one's time; but they appear to enjoy it.*

On my own end, I am reminded of something which I, myself, have never forgotten: *it is a constant struggle not to become what others believe you to be.* And if they believe you to be evil, you sometimes need to ask yourself, "Why bother fighting it? Be the evil they see in you. Do unto them – and with great fury."

Anyone half-sane mind needs to ask:

*Why are you battling to hold back the instincts which scream for you to lash out, to attack, to be the monster they claim you are? Why don't you hurt them before they kill you for "being" something you're not?*

The answer is that I have no intention of letting them define me, not even when I might benefit from it. To project an identity onto another is to attempt to remove that person's soul. It is an assault on the self, which is worse than an assault on the body. (Not that the two are far interchanged—if your purpose is to break my leg, it's also to break my spirit, no?)

Some beings live their entire lives without even wondering about what's inside; it never occurs to them that they could be other than what they've been told they are. Contrariwise, some try to assume roles which are easily understood from the outside, so that other sentients don't have to think too hard in order to "figure you out".

Action is aided and abetted by that same damn pattern recognition, the one that prompts both insight, and delusion. It takes a great deal of processing power to assess a new thing as if it were unique. The more you question the world around you, the more brainpower you need to apply to what you do. So very many pieces of our lives can fit into reasonable algorithms of habit. If you stop questioning the patterns, you *become* only your habits, no more able to break free of them than a reflection can step away from its mirror.

How do you deal with something which is very similar to, but distinct from, that which is covered by your existing coping mechanisms? One method is to nudge, or cut, or burn, or carve, or otherwise alter the new thing, until it's essentially identical to the old thing–and then you have a working system again.

This is why humans mutilate stuff; not out of sadism, but because they fear it until they've hacked it into a recognizable shape.

Creating understanding new? That's much harder. And it's suspect, as well. If someone's going to be a functional member of society, why would that person do things which question or challenge that society? Oh, sure, from an intellectual standpoint, we understand that change comes from difference; but *you* try walking around in your werewolf form instead of your human shape, and see what happens. "Stop running," you shout, "Lycanthropy has many benefits! It strengthens your immune system, helps you heal, *and* lets you eat your meat without the inconvenience of cooking!" But do they listen? Nope.

Even if you don't *intend* to be a threat, consider the idea that *you are anyway*. Societies need misfits for advancement; but those same misfits tend to cause unpredictability, and sometimes catastrophic system failure. Sometimes they do it on purpose.

I can't say this often enough, because it's both very true, and not at all intuitive to me: the unusual is a threat. I don't feel it as keenly as others, I think, partly because I don't spend much time around other humans, and partly because I've always felt *drawn* to the unusual. Which sounds desirable, until you figure that it's why there's currently an entire army sallying forth to silence my curiosity with maximum permanence.

This is a simple logical proposition. It's not any sort of complicated intuitive leap. Societies respond to anomalies much as bodies answer infections: through illness, and a desire to drive the malady *out*.

That's why they hate us.

That's why they *have* to hate us.

We either need to teach ourselves to fit in, or we need to teach them how to care about and respect us.

Or, perhaps, just perhaps, there's a third option: The lesson that certain kinds of fears are best faced, not with a mob of adrenaline-fueled temporary allies, but by turning aside while you yet live.

# ON CORRUPTION

---

Dear Chosen One,

As we near what is likely to be the end of our acquaintance, and one of our lives, I'm going to give you a bit more advice. If all goes well for you, and I hope it does not, you might stand next to a ruler soon. Let me tell you something about proximity to power.

It's a little glib to say that all power corrupts. Far more accurate to say that power *changes* you—or at least, creates inevitable alterations of your environment and will not permit you to stand still.

For example, assume that the power of your side increases, and you somehow remain completely as you were. If so, *someone* will wield the new force, and if it is not you, then you create a vacuum. Either *your* side uses it, or it goes away, to be snapped up by some opponent or new player.

If it's *not* seized by an opponent, then it will be seized by an underling. This often will not go well for you; an ambitious subordinate who gains puissance may not choose to remain subordinate. And the nearest throne to seize is usually yours.

Besides, if you pick up the reins of greater power and remain unchanged inside, *it will not matter*. Because as long as those around you know you have increased, they will act on it. In some, it will bring out the flatterer; in some, the schemer. In even the conscientious, there will be a desire to fill your mind with good news, so as never to run the risk of telling you unpleasant truths. Perhaps you have given them no reason to believe that you'll meet bad news with punishment; but even the best will say, "Things are different now; why take the risk?" Soon, you will find it nearly impossible to know what is going on around you—and they will scorn you (but not quite to your face) for being unapproachable and out of touch.

Power changes how you are seen; and whether or not it actually corrupts you, others will assume it has. Which is, as far as I'm concerned, worse.

If, as in my case, you do not really have day-to-day subordinates (I have solitude, allies, and magic; that's more than enough to manage)--then it is your enemies who will hear that you are stronger, and fear you, and thereby hate you in new and special ways.

Have no enemies? Wait until you have gained enough power; that'll change. Fast.

And thus, power does not simply give you the ability to change; it *requires* you to do so. Because you will be seen as tainted, and even doing precisely what you did before will yield unexpectedly different results. Your environment evolves around you; evolve with it, or it will leave you behind. And in all cases, they will see you as a beast.

Do you know the difference between perceived as evil, and actually *being* evil?

*Hint: It doesn't actually matter to those who are looking for a reason to slit your throat.*

# Some Things To Remember About Pain

Pain is fuel, meant to be ruthlessly converted into inspiration.

Granted, hurt is not necessarily a pleasant or desirable muse. It doesn't always inspire beauty; it doesn't even always inspire something functional. In fact, that's part of the challenge of pain–trying to use raw ugliness to shape something that will fit into a world which prefers the aesthetically pleasing.

One response is simply to ignore pain. That is sometimes what it teaches you–to keep going in spite of the hurt. Contrariwise, sometimes the hurt is a thing you really *need* to understand, and you force it away at your own peril. It's not fun, telling which is which.

The Chosen One is currently experiencing much discomfort. Not really *pain*, per se. A small stab wound from an Orcish knife. An inordinately pokey rock for a pillow. It's just your standard camping trip on the way to eradicate evil.

I do not envy her the unpleasantness she'll come to know. I've done no augury, but by instinct, I'd predict what comes next is the loss of comrades or allies–some through death, some through misfortune, and, worst and least expected–some because they find out they don't really want to live in the shadow of someone "special".

The Chosen One and I share this thing: people are happiest to see us leave. Some see her as a savior; some see me as a leader; but even those don't really see *either* of us as someone with whom you'd have a drink.

(Joke's on them; more wine for us, eh?)

There is surprisingly little difference between the deference shown to a tyrant king, and the kindness shown to a prophesied creature. One commands loyalty through hypothetical terror and force, one through supposed virtue and a mission which will "save" them all.

The truth is, they fear us both.

The Chosen One seems kindly and empathic. I find her very likable, though I'm not looking forward to her attempt to massacre me. And all the villagers of all the little hamlets smile at her, and they praise her, and they offer her gifts.

And they're so glad when she leaves.

Because world-changing destiny is never a comfort. No matter how bad you find the Universe around you, being a pattern-maker is part of human sentience, and therefore, the thought that someone will wreck the familiar shapes of one's world is horrible. That's true even--perhaps *especially*--if you *hate* the way the world is now. No matter that she's making that wreckage for your benefit.

The familiar will become strange. Perhaps it's strange in good ways, perhaps we acknowledge that the world's a better place, but few are really comfortable around world-changers. Because *who knows what they'll change next?*

# The Unfortunate Magic of Love

Now, the Sagas would find you hooking up, somewhere along your journey, with some sweet love.

But that's not the fate for our kind, O Chosen One.

Love is not more magical than hate, nor does it last longer. Nor does the former even feel better than the latter emotion, necessarily. But hate is more fitting sometimes. It grants you a vast and terrible freedom: You can do almost anything to destroy that which stands in front of you, because you are certain in your heart that it is wrong.

Whereas love? Love is constraining; love is all the things you cannot do because you're obligated to another. Do not be surprised when hatred feels like what it is: freedom. And don't be surprised when Love feels like what is—sometimes: a cage.

To love is to give yourself to another, which is noble and beautiful, when done between the right people at the right time. But when declared simply from strong feeling in a given moment, as though it were some self-evident truth, it is terrifying. "I love you" says "I want to be one with you". This can be a merging of souls; but it can also be the pure hunger of soul cannibalism.

Love is not, as some weaker beings think, contemptible, a flaw, a thing to be avoided. Love likewise does not make you weak; love joins you to another, making you both strong.

If you both know what that love is. **If** it means the same thing to both of you. If it actually joins you together, rather than attaching one of you like a limpet mine to another who is not necessarily ready, willing, able, excited, or even capable of pinning two fates together.

Love is no more all-powerful than hunger, or the desire to re-produce. But we often assign enough gravity to shift a planetary orbit to what is frequently no more than a mating call.

Love is potentially deadly, because we expect it to be the end of a search, the meaning of a journey, the answer to some very ulti-mate questions—and it is, instead, a long, sharp set of questions. Sometimes you find answers that work. Sometimes you realize you were an idiot to ask in the first place.

Hormones are natural things, Chosen One; but making signifi-cant change in the world is, by definition, nothing like natural. We have priorities which contradict our glands, and if glands don't like it, that's their misfortune.

# DIARY OF THE CHOSEN ONE: HOW TO KILL A DARK LORD

It's taken a long time, but I think I have it. If my researches are correct—and admittedly, that's a large hope, considering that I'm an amateur doing complex esoteric magical research with approximately zero assistance from the staff-waving mage guy who's nominally my guide—the Dark Lord keeps heart, unsurprisingly, separate from body.

The White Wizard claims that he's always known this, but it was essential to my path that I discover it for myself. I might believe him if, first, he wasn't a pathological liar, and second, I hadn't tested him by initially saying "Harp" instead of "Heart".

(He then proceeded to go on a five-minute diatribe about how it was obviously clear that we needed to find the correct song to play upon it, and how we'd need to find a bard. When I confronted him with the truth, he looked squirrely for a moment, then said, "Actually, ahem, I meant a metaphor, as in heart-strings, and..." – but by then, I'd stopped caring.)

Fortunately, and not coincidentally, there is a vast amount of scholarship, folklore, and study on the subject. This isn't a new spell, or even an unusual one. What distinguishes this version is likely not any thaumaturgical originality, but what must be extraordinary strength, focus, and control.

You see, enabling long life through an enchanted aorta is a well-known, if difficult, enchantment. You start by infusing the thing with some amount of essence, soul, and power; that's not simply to preserve those things in the case of bodily death, but also because any fleshly vessel, no matter how augmented, can only store so much force and stand so much modification before it demonstrates what a lightning storm would look like if it started inside of skin and worked its way violently outward.

*Ergo, channeling the kind of spellcraft we've seen from the Dark Lord—and we've presumably only seen a fraction of it—from Word, to mind, to body, to a heart maintained outside the body, then back to the body again—would fry just about anyone like a particularly misfortunate kipper. Most enchanters who've used some version of this hex have, according to their own diaries, essentially retired, gaining longer lives at the expense of removing the ability to do all but the most basic magic.*

*(And I feel like they wouldn't lie about this; why else fill your memoir with demonic encounters, vast weatherworkings, and the divination of nigh-unknowable Names, only to have the last chapters be infrequent entries about how well or poorly your tomatoes are growing and why the price of firewood is too damn high?)*

*Removing a vital organ and investing it with the stuff of your life is a vulnerability, of course. The thing would hold a great deal of power and (perhaps) parts of your soul. Such an object could be destroyed by the right kind of magical item.*

*And I've seen more than my share of those; apparently, part of the job description of "Chosen One" means galloping all over the damn landscape in search of magical items. (Hint: Many ensorcelled things are much less useful than one would like. Bags which hold more things than they ought to tend to be hungry, and go snapping after spare change, shiny stuff, and fingers. Seven-league boots have a preference for landing you face-first in trees and rocks. And swords? It's true what they say; the more powerful the sword, the more it seeks to cut things open. Anything. And anyone. In essence, most magic doesn't attach itself to an object for the pleasure of the random person who might pick it up. Magic not actively controlled by a sentient's will tends to impose its own will on the world. It took forever for me to put a usable hex on my dagger, and even then, I suspect can draw it approximately once before it'll essentially begin choosing its own targets.)*

*In short, The Dark Lord must needs reinvest into (and, perhaps, do battle with) that heart on a regular basis. Which means that it's kept outside of the body, but nearby.*

*Hell, I do much the same with my own heart, no magic required. I mean, why does magic rebel? Because few of us really want to be nothing more than a tool.*

*"Do this, Chosen One."*

*"Be this, Chosen One."*

"Give us this thing, and this thing. Turn your head so the populace can see you. Bend your head low so that the Orcs cannot." I do what they say. I do my job.

But I do not become theirs.

I must be the Chosen One, but I will also remain myself. Maybe they don't understand this. That's their problem.

My own heart doesn't like the mask, the role. It is frustrated and dissenting, and sometimes, it whispers in the dark. And that voice isn't some devil or tempter; it's my own voice.

My heart is a secret, powerful thing.

Dark Lord, I know how it feels.

# THE DESTRUCTION OF THE GREAT LIBRARY

As mentioned before, sometimes someone with reason to consult the archives of a nation or place will express...*frustration*...that we know so little of our past.

Humans have a helpful myth, though. Once there was a Great Library. And great it was *indeed*! It was splendid, stuffed fuller than a holiday waterfowl with sages, white of beard and saintly of eyes, and it simply had *all* the books on all of everything. And then one day, one fell day, The Monster just came and burned it to the ground.

Which monster? Oddly enough, accounts seems to vary, depending on who tells the tale. One bit's clear, though: it was never the fault of the side recounting the legend.

You catch a theme? Forgive me if I belabor it. But it's this:

If two or three people tell a given story about an event, and are believed, then that affects the perceptions of those around them. Humans are highly subject to confirmation bias. If a few people are loud enough in saying that "these people are Good; those beings are Darkness incarnate!" – then, in many minds, it become so, regardless of what the other beings have done or what they are. Eventually, it becomes their truth. I reflect on this often, particularly because spellwork requires attempting to understand how Names are made, and the construction of the name "monster" in particular is of extraordinary import.

*Consider:* A young child spies a Goblin near a human settlement, looking at the human habitation with wonder and wistful yearning. The youth might be puzzled and feel moved to empathy by the pain on that darkling's face. But wait until the child speaks of this to parents, who immediately yell at their offspring, and then cart the kid over to the town square, which is full of neighbors. They surround the child; this one shows an eye lost to Goblin attack (he speaks not of who attacked whom first, nor of the war around them, but surely that doesn't matter, eh?) That one speaks of arriving only in the nick of time to prevent a Goblin from stealing her crops of wheat. (Goblins are actually gluten intolerant, but few people know that, and besides, who cares?) Everyone,suddenly,has a tale to tell. Her peers begin taking up makeshift toy swords and shields, vowing to defend the village. One kid refuses to play, and they torment her, calling her a monster herself, and saying that she sides with predators against the village.

In less time than you would think, the original spotter-of-Goblins has resolved that what she observed was a most definite look of cunning and hatred. The creature she saw wasn't quietly observing a human settlement as a sad outsider, looking in; it was planning incursion! Maybe she even noticed signs in the distance that there were more Goblins, just beyond the tree-line—no doubt armed to the teeth. She's lucky to have caught it when she did.

And this is what she will tell her friends.

And the lie spins 'round another cycle or two...

It's often said that humans are inherently good. Oh, they sometimes do bad things, but most of the time that's just the occasional warring enemy tribe, and a good chronicling will show that misfits were properly wiped out. (By the grace of Gods, o' course, who are very much on the side of those who commanded that a given saga be written down. It's fascinating how much humans put words into the mouths of Gods. One would think the Gods might resent it. Of course, the God who disapproves of you must, surely, be a Dark God...

.... worshipped only by your enemies. Ahem.)

Whereas, in contrast, virtuous humans are the inheritors of wisdom, progenitors of veracity. They are the beacon of brightness in what is an otherwise gloomy, hostile, and unfriendly universe.

And if you believe that, we've got a bridge to Narnia we can sell you. Cheap.

I became a Dark Lord because I knew that I wanted to effect change not like a *homo sapiens*, not like part of the human cycle of victory and erasure. I wanted to step outside of those history books, become some kind of thing unto myself. There have been a few Dark Lords, each one different, each one barely beaten, if at all (some just...slumber. Some seem to have found ways to as-

cend to the moon or descend into the seas, and simply have nothing more to do with Man. I am more foolish—I could call it 'au-
dacious' if I felt like flattering myself—and I have my own ideas
on where I might live. Somewhere beautiful and endless—like the
eternal Goblin song, perhaps.).

The strongest defense against being rewritten when you die is
to avoid dying, of course. II could have taken a path more likely to
keep me alive, and I'd have been less of a target. But vanishing off
the map leaves you in no real position to go changing what's *on* the
map. So it's rather unhelpful if you care about the world of Man,
and I do. Sometimes I care in ways that make me want to raze said
world to the ground; but if that's not a human feeling, what is?

It is no comfort, but also no surprise, that the White Wizard and
the Chosen One have found one of the few paths to my cessation,
and they carry it with them. It is part of why their visit is not precisely heartwarming to me.

Some scholars suggest that one can best understand the motivations of humanity as a whole by seeing it as a response the
grave. Whatever we desire, whatever we want, we are are tempo-
rally bound, and deeply finite. That cuts particularly deeply into
one who can, in many other areas, make reality malleable. Some of
it is practical: we might have to die, but not as soon as others of
our species. But then we get to an ugly little problem: if we pro-
long our allotted time on this planet, how do we deal with the feelings of others who live much shorter lives?

Oh, you could shut out everyone else. You could decide that
every opposing voice is badly broken and sadly mistaken. You
could seek to quell every possibility of dissent. You could make a
unity of thought—a hivemind--or you could search for so much
control that none could speak against you. But in doing all of these
things you duck out of understanding yourself, and build in a lovely little fatal flaw. You do yourself a disservice by pretending that
extended life is unending life. Because *mortality is urgency,ur-
gency is energy*. With it, we could push hard enough to move the
world; without it, it's hard to remember why one should bother to
get out of bed.

When the world doesn't fit your notions of it, *question your notions*. Believing that the problem lies with the world, and not the
story you tell yourself, is so quaint, so insane, and so utterly human; it's charming, sad, and horrifying.

There was never a Great Library, no assemblage of all human knowledge; there are humans, trying desperately to make sense of the world, and forever thwarting themselves at doing so.

# A TURNING TIDE BOILS THE SEA

Humans get to live inside the knowledge that they are special. It's a lovely place to be. Why not imagine that you are precious and unique, regardless of what you do?

This sounds like the beginning of a criticism, and it's true, as the armies of Men come to slaughter me, I do not have the warmest of fuzzy feelings for my species.

But let's be honest. The human psyche is a tremendously complex thing, and in some ways a tremendously fragile thing. It takes in what you tell it, and it makes of that a set of principles, a foundation, an architecture of rationalization.

I can't say whether this is the product of how we create the technology of culture, or whether it's an offshoot of culture itself. But I can't fault it. The more you recognize the scope of the Universe, the more difficult it is to have a real capacity for thinking that you might be doing something horribly wrong. And if you've reached a point in your society when you might have to face the idea that this isn't an isolated incident, or a particular moment, or some atrocity committed under the reign of some inauspicious King—that it's possible *things have been broken for a real long time*—then life becomes quite difficult.

How many can stand up to the idea that *they* might be the reason we cannot have nice things?

Most can't. Most don't.

And so they comfort themselves with tautology: Good must, and shall, prevail, because it is good. After that, they just add a broad assumption: "Good" lies on their side of the fence, "Evil" on the other.

We'll see how well that works out for them.

Meanwhile, I'll marshal my defenses.

The White Wizard claims that I have called forth every creature of the Dark. He is approximately...oh, ten percent right, though he'll never understand that.

To be perfectly honest, I asked most of them *not* to defend me. I pointed out that it was a suicide mission for the vast majority of them, and while we had some plans, this might not be the right place, the right time, the right moment. I've been scrying the White Wizard's path for a long time, and it's sewn with the corpses of beings like the ones who now guard my castle. I'm not looking for death, nor do I prefer my cessation to that of others; I'd like to live, and I'm fine if someone else has to die for it. But I'd rather that those who die not be my friends. It's not because I'm "good". It's because friendship is especially meaningful when you've dwelt, for many many years, alone and in the dark.

I've been making preparations for more than the lifespan of the average human, and my aversion almost feels like cowardice. *But I just want more time.* It's too soon. I don't like this fight.

They things of the Dark have spent a great deal of time preparing for the day they would fight humanity. It was not the wisest of ideas, but they *really* wanted this. They wanted what they saw as their chance to win back the Sun. I wanted to tell them their force of arms was not likely to carry the battle; it's all very well and good to spend generations sharpening your daggers, teaching your young that someday, you will swarm forth from your places of exile. But that doesn't match up with the way our respective species work. Humans attach to the ever-growing war effort about the same importance that other species would attach to the war effort, plus everything else that species is seeking to do at a given time, anywhere, ever.

Man the toolmaker, Man the builder of incredible things, Man whose peoples will spend decades making nothing but slightly-better catapults!

This is part of the nature of our kind. To grow through conquest--of land, of sea, of other beings. Does that make us less ethical than beings which stick more to themselves? Hard to say. If you were to pit a Human scholar against a scholar of the Orcs to discuss morality, you'd quickly find that the human scholar would stab the Orc and the debate would end.

So the question goes unanswered.

And in that sense humans are stunted, because ideas in human worlds blow up, like magma spewing out of an overactive volcano. Humans are gifted; they're builders and constructors of ideas. We're great dreamers; and thus great liars. We make wonders no-one would believe, which is part of why it's so easy to tell lies that are equally unbelievable. Hew mighty rocks into an astrologically-predictive circle with stone-age tools? Seems impossible, but we've done it. Orcs don't speak, they just kill? Seems impossible, but the monolith-builders said it was true, and who are we to question them?

Fairy tales could come true. It could happen to you. If you work your ass off. Or you imprison the fairy and mention casually that you will be removing its wings if it does not alter its tale, and what it believes to be the truth.

# WHY SO MANY TORTURERS ARE IDIOTS

There's so much more I want to know about humans (and about everything.) I've wanted to undertake many experiments on my species, but I hesitate. I am the product of, if not human experimentation, then certainly some of humanity's most transformative practices. You get good data taking an innocent and pouring shoving demons down his throat; but the data's always flawed.

I don't often resort to capture, much less harrowing those in my possession. These are practical matters: if you torture something, you either destroy its value, or—if it survives, even as a broken thing—it comes out stronger. The former makes enemies from whom you can take no profit; the latter creates those who are now tempered enough to do you real harm.

Realistically, in order to accrue a net gain, you need to have a serious enjoyment of the misery of others before you start to exert cruelty upon them; if that personal hedonic value isn't there, then the cost is just too high. It's impractical, because you are making an antagonist for life. And if you believe the one you torture will simply never escape, and will just die in captivity, you ought to consider the stimulating effects agony has upon the brain. Start with someone meek and mild, inflict torment upon them, and sure, some will die or break. But a certain percentage will stop being clinically depressed, and start being monomaniacally focused on ending you. You want those people dead; you want them never to have existed at all, if possible. You most certainly don't want to create *more* of them, even in cages. *Especially* in cages.

And even if you enjoy the distress of others, it's an expensive pleasure. It takes a fairly short period of pleasant dissolution for entropy and chaos to erode your resources and leave you with nothing. There's a part of an Archmage's mind which asks—rightly,

I believe—"You have world-spanning powers; why are you wasting them poking holes in this poor bastard's central nervous system?" It's like owning a mighty war-horse for the sole purpose of having others paint it into pictures with you.

Revenge is a famous theme in our lives. It has a certain poetic justice. It allows us to engage in the depths of sadism without taking on the weight of doing evil; those who've wronged you sufficiently deserve to pay, pay, pay, don't they?

And it deters others from harming you, at least temporarily, at least sometimes.

But I don't like it as a path. In fact, I've been known to avoid it at my peril. This isn't because I'm a hero. It's because anger, while often a powerful fuel, is also a wasteful thing. Revenge is like a plate of sugar-cookies; each one gives you a rush, but it's hard to stop at one, and if you go through the whole plate, your stomach will despise you. Revenge for the sake of revenge takes a toll on anyone; I should know; I have enemies who feel I deserve the worst retribution. They seldom succeed in even the nascent parts of their plans, though. Because while they're out trying to burn the last thing I did, I'm building something newer, and I'm building it out of fire-proof stone. Their fury limits their thinking (which, if you ask me, might not have been their finest attribute to begin with.)

It takes a certain anger, or a certain blindness, to do unto others as they have done unto you, especially in specific, one-to-one situations. Like I said, feels great—but do you really need it? They call me monstrous; well, I guess I am. I don't need to look good to them, and I don't need to get rid of the ones who won't sing my praises. I'm not a damned Unicorn. I may always have been ugly, but I'm proud of it. I don't need to disfigure others to show them how to understand me. If they don't understand me, and they fight me, then they fight with a grave disadvantage, and they likely die; they believe me to be other than what I am, *less* than what I am, and they don't prepare for what I can do, what I can survive.

Underestimation is narcotic: it lulls you into a sense of well-being, while dulling your ability to perceive new sources of pain.

Personally, I'm fine if my enemies believe their own stories about me. But I'd rather, for myself, hear more truth about my enemies and myself, than flattering lies. Knowledge is power; egotism is weakness. That's why being hit by unpleasant reality matters much more to me than having some prisoner, some enemy, or some craven magic mirror say, "No, you're beautiful, I swear!"

\*

# True Believers

*They have crossed the border into my lands. They're burning every-thing in their path, and they are nearly here.*

(Memo to self: The next time you think you have enough whiskey on hand, remember that you're wrong.)

Humans can think, unlike mere beasts, which can only react. My favorite theory about how this came to pass is that, in the early days of Creation, the critters of land and sea bribed the *hell* out of whatever gods were handing out brains.

Thinking beings are quantitatively different from other animals in their psychologies. To take a relatively specific subset, there are a few famous examples of sentience being given to creatures through magic or alchemy. It's commonly known that most of those creatures are, at best, bitter with the world. Sentience has not been a boon to them. Why would it be? Make the Sphynx con-scious, tell her to stand forever at a crossroads, ask passers-by a difficult question, and eat the ones who answer poorly. This is not going to be a well-adjusted individual.

Going from nonsentience to cognizance is not a pleasant awak-ening. I don't know of anyone who's ever solved the conundrum of "Is it better to be happy, or smart?" That's partly because it's a broken phrase, though it sounds good. It's more helpful to ask "Is it better to see too little of the world, possibly missing opportuni-ties—or to see enough of the world that you recognize how large, frightening, and painful it could be?" The imagination needed to make worthwhile things also brings you an idea of just how awful the future might be.

This is why newly-thinking beings often seek to harm them-selves and others. Part of understanding the world is realizing that agency is often linked to tearing down barriers, breaking chains, smashing walls, becoming something more and different and *other* than what was expected of you. Indeed, if you really wish to achieve purpose you *must* act out. You *must* wonder if you have misnamed something you defined. You *must* question your own narratives, or you will make your own echo chamber, and no-one can rescue you from it, because it is stuck inside your own head.

It would be interesting to take a number of renegade Humans and a group of Orcs who simply reject broken histories, and give them a chance to make their own way and their own laws. Perhaps they might, in time, establish a kingdom of savage purpose and joyous naming. Humans are more creative than anyone; hyperactive enthusiastic monkey-critters, excitedly chittering about everything, and picking up this bit to see if it fits against that bit. And Orcs understand patience, and though their spirit is burnt from being hunted, it's also lifted up by the knowledge that no pain endures forever.

What a team you might have!

If they ever stopped trying to kill each other.

But so far, that's never happened.

I don't know what will come next. I don't think anyone does. Humans believe they'll be saved if they take me down; I wish I could warn them about the White Wizard. But my chance of being heard is long gone; I could present the clearest of proofs, and it would be disregarded by most as vile hedge-wizard tricks.

And so there's not much to do but wait, brew a few more spells, and listen to the rhythmic stomping of many kinds of boots, right outside the walls of my Keep. My fortress is, of necessity, built into a mountain; no infantry will take us from that direction, nor from the sides. The front has been stripped of trees and forest so that my Orcish archers have clear lines of sight.

Soon, the land around me will be decorated with corpses. I have always preferred those oil paintings of dogs playing card games, myself. But it's not really my choice anymore.

*And now comes Man, with banner raised*
*And now comes Man, a God appraised*
*(By his own, impeccably certain mind*
*The one that makes him slightly blind.)*
*Will there be deaths? O, deaths a-plenty*
*And bodies burning consequently*
*And once the war is over and done*
*All glory to the Chosen One.*

# A Dark Lord's Apology

*You think; therefore, you think you be. You build this hope from fear:*
*You think, if you think ill of me, I'll simply disappear.*
*Tear down my works, tear down my name - and think that makes me gone*
*But, in fact, I'll return to claim: Your sky, your moon--*
*Your dawn.*

I have waited for this day for a very long time, with both hunger and dread. I'm glad this day has come; I wish this day hadn't come yet.

Because even after I spent all of these missives denying the force of what others wish to impose upon me, I can't deny that the pressure is incredibly powerful. We're made of bones, spirit, and dreams. But they are often other people's dreams, and they're often the bones that others have sharpened into spears to pierce your spirit and bleed it out.

I think that for my whole life, or at least as soon as I was conscious enough have that tiny kernel which is sense of self, I wanted. I craved. I desired. I *needed* to name myself, to say, "This thing is what I am. The words you have for me? They are not accurate. Let me show you another way to view a misfit.".

It's not about whether good beats evil or evil beats good; it's about the way the words which best shape reality beat *everything*. But there is so *much* consensus reality among so many humans, so much unshakable conviction that if many people believe it, it must be true. So much of that, so little of me. Sometimes I think I'm an idiot for trying to get anyone to believe difficult truths rather than easy lies.

I'm sorry for how much my allies have been endangered.

I'm sorry that I wasn't smart enough to figure out some way of trying to get free without shedding so much blood.

**I am sorry for the trolls, awkward, slow, inexorable, coming forth from their places of pretending to be rock formations, forming a living wall around my castle.** I am certain that they will fall to ingenious machines and sheer weight of numbers. But they will thin the ranks of those who've come to tear down my works, and to them, that is enough.

I don't think any of the trolls expect to survive this. Perhaps some of them realize that they can pit their strength and clubs almost equally against engines of war. But they know they can't stand long before humans. Trolls may be sluggish of mind, but they recognize ruthless, unstoppably naked ambition, and they know its name: "Man".

I think that many beings of the Dark have come to recognize that what humans see as the spark of "heroism" is a self-brewed intoxicant, and they realize how viciously murderous it makes those in whose veins it burns. In truth, that flickering ember is life force, which flows through all conscious beings. Humans have merely weaponized it, and their internal flame sparks higher and hotter than most, because they feel absolutely entitled to it. This, despite the fact that they assuredly don't know what the hell it is. They're certain it comes from the Gods as a gift to them; if you told them that all of us possess it, they'd label you a heretic. And possibly do some whining to their Gods.

Don't like mysticism? Don't prefer Divinities, even in a world of magic? Understandable. Call it, if you prefer, not a gift from beings Celestial, but something else: a potentiation of our ability to think, combined with our ability to will. Every fool knows that holy, mystical, even philosophical books speak of a "power that comes from within"; we've heard it so many times that we make it a part of bad children's stories: "And lo, at the moment when she needed it most, she found the force within her. She didn't find it in time to avoid having her head bitten off, but she sure died enlightened."

(All right. Perhaps not everyone tells children's stories the way I do. But gallows humor continues to be the prerogative of those likely to die.)

We tend to disregard the will to power as being the province of certain philosophers, as poorly-constructed fiction, or as wishful thinking. Sometimes we attribute it entirely to some exterior force, make it into something granted *to* you, rather than starting inside. But there are thresholds at which we're able to exceed our theoretical reach, breaking through barriers and achieving the thought-to-be-impossible. We find it easiest to do this in groups, because the simplest way to fly past the boundaries of your own beliefs is to have a thousand others, all screaming the same idea, loudly enough that you don't have time to disbelieve it. And it's not always something shining with glory. For example, mobs are made of this force, catalyzed by the seductive pheromones of mass anger, and in that form, this energy is rightly famous for leading to acts of exceptional bravery, stupidity, and brutality.

We distrust these things on an individual level because it smacks too much of Godhead; it's threatening to see a single person, or a small group of people, do something in defiance of what "everyone" knows is achievable. But that is the Making Machine, the great forge of sentience. It's the heritage of all beings who think: to be able to bring into the world that which never previously had shape or form. If you asked me, I would tell you that trying to suppress that energy on an individual level is a shame. Trying to do so for a nation or culture is, simply, a crime. But what they *actually* criminalize is the act of breaking free and defying conventional ideas.

They *will* kill you for it.

*If they can.*

**The trolls fall like the giant rocks they aren't.** Wholesale slaughter. I hope not every one of them came forth from the Dark; I hope these were not the very last of their race. Trolls are a very practical species for such slow-moving, thoughtful creatures. And oddly enough, moving a little like glaciers, thinking slow bass-note thoughts like ancient trees, they yet decided to be here. Others might have sent no-one; why risk the remains of a species on likely death?

Unless they decided that it wasn't risk. Unless they decided it was a simple, logical proposition to end all at once, with purpose—rather than be slowly driven out from every hiding place by those who steal the light.

That's a bit different from the Orcs, who simply sent an all-or-nothing army. For their beliefs are simpler:

They *will* find the Sun. They *will* drive the humans from it. At least for a time. That is their intent. But even if they succeed, I worry about what will happen next. Because they underestimate- -all nonhumans underestimate--human fanaticism. No one can match Humanity when it comes to glorious causes, beautiful ideas, and the mass death of whoever's currently causing them discomfort.

Some of the trolls are, in fact, stumbling off the field of battle, badly hurt but alive. The human forces are thinned. They fire arrow after arrow at the wounded stone beasts, but it's early in the day, and the very Sun itself is in the Archers' eyes. As if it were no longer their ally. Or as if it existed for more than just their convenience.

But that's impossible, of course.

# On Inhumanity: Yet Another Letter To The Chosen One

Dearest Chosen One:

You're quite near your destination, which is to say, me. I am leaving this missive in your mind. And I have, in turn, received the last several you sent me. I'm sorry; I initially mistook them for ordinary nightmares.

You live an unenviable life. You have my condolences. Even if you survive.

I've been composing my thoughts. I didn't write this one for you, but you get to have it anyway; if the White Wizard burns all of my notebooks, you'll remain as a final repository of some of my knowledge.

Don't tell him. I feel like it wouldn't brighten his day.

The Wizard, as he has said more than once, believes that I have left humanity behind, and am now some other thing altogether. Or perhaps I never was human; that would make things simpler, wouldn't it?

I don't care what the Wizard thinks—assuming that calcified set of prewritten assumptions of his can even be called "thought". But *you*, Chosen. You know what it's like to be made out of questions. Do *you* believe that? Believe I'm some other thing altogether? That I left my heritage behind when I shook off the hatreds which drove me away in the first place? I know I repeat myself about this, and I hate it. But if other people questioned your humanity daily, you'd find yourself looking for some kind of feedback, yourself. "I think I'm human. I seem to be human. What does this person know about me that I'm missing?"

It's an insane tale, to me. It would be strange to work so hard, only to make myself into, not something *different*, but some parody, some weird perversion of humanity. How nonsensical to pour my blood and life energy into simply becoming a caricature, no true thing in and of herself, but simply an aberrant version of the heroes!

Why would I be that thing?

Even if I could, *why would I desire it?*

Why take on the stale magic of others, simply in the hope that if I pervert it sufficiently, I can do something new with it—*rather than create magic of my own?*

Yeah, making your own thing is more difficult, but it's also *yours*. Why take credit for what you *didn't* do? For that matter, why accept rewards you can't use, or more succinctly, why take dominion without a plan? Governing the lives of thousands or millions doesn't self-organize.

It's shortsighted fools who don't look beyond gaining control. Distrust anyone whose entire rationale for becoming a monarch is "Once the Kingdom is mine, I will wear a crown, and it will be terribly shiny." Why would someone who is searching for the deepest secrets of Magic be particularly excited at gaining a kingdom? The time drain of running things in the mortal world is a hindrance, not a help, to research; and what is the fear and awe of an enslaved populace, which is a cheap and plentiful commodity, compared to the raw joys of making change in the Multiverse?

And also, once you get to that whole "King" or "Empress" deal, you'll find out firsthand that sure, the throne offers power, but it also invites the likelihood that a percentage of your wine goblets will also contain an annoying arsenic cocktail.

Sure, you could dwell in that lone tower with the trappings of your might and your inscrutably pleasing toys, perhaps be mysterious and rarely seen. But then the populace encounters you mainly in times of trouble, which hardly inspires loyalty, especially if some of their problems came about because you were too busy chasing the Elixir of Life to do something about that cattle flu.

There's a temptation to be inefficiently despotic because it's easy—for a while, at least, as you live off whatever resources accumulated before you came to power, and you can always try to subvert and destroy other kingdoms, take their stuff, and start using *that* up. Heck, do it long enough, and other rulers will accept you as kin; you may be weird, but at least you're acting just like they do. But that's an idiotic plan for anyone who's interested in having a future.

I became Dark Lord partly to get *away* from the incessant influence of those who perpetually tried to shape me into something I'm not. I don't plan to give in to them now.

I do think my chances of survival are poor. Almost everything which opposes humanity dies, because in the end, humanity has unparalleled skill at tearing things down. (Sure, they can also lift up things no other species have attempted; but that's not a side of them I see much, these days. Neither do they; they don't seem to care what gets knocked down when they come after me, as long as they end me.)

I suppose I've always been something a bit alien, even when I was a little child. Finding forbidden magic seemed a natural step for someone who always felt out of place; it wasn't until years later that I found out that many kids feel that the same displacement, have the same sense of being out of touch with the world. Most of them do *not*, however, choose to express it by seeking out hidden and terrible lore, apparently. It's too much like homework.

(Not everyone, of course. There are plenty of humans who have no desire for what lies ahead, or who passed through childhood no more beloved than I, but who became artists or healers or people who just raise families well and treat others with decency. I feel bad that they're caught up in any of this madness. But when enough humans decide to unite in stupidity, the effects are terribly far-reaching.)

And sometimes, I feel that very little has changed since my childhood. Then, as now, there seem to be an exceptionally large number of people who just can't quite figure out how to wake up and get motivated in the morning if they have to face their own errors and mistakes, the flaws in their judgment, the pain brought on them through their actions of malice or foolishness. Much better to have a scapegoat, particularly one who isn't anywhere near the taverns where you're expressing your displeasure. My name grows in every telling; after all, the man who says he's been cursed, that his cow bred a two-headed calf, has his drinks bought for him all night. How would his neighbor resist saying, "Oh, I, as well—in fact, my calf was born with three heads, and a most alarming facial expression, to boot; fill me up, kind barkeep"?

Why did I become Dark Lord? Because I didn't choose to affect change like a human. I chose to do something grander, stranger, more threatening to some of humanity's ideals.

Now we go reap some consequences.

**Orcish swords, sharpened over generations, glint for a moment before being covered in blood which darkens them from point to hilt.** It goes not well for the armies of Man. The human army is larger than all the forces arrayed against it. Better trained. More united. More experienced. Even their weapons are better.

But they had poor expectations.

They believed they'd see anger, fear, and perhaps disgust. They also had the great disadvantage of Destiny—that is, they clearly went in thinking there was no possible outcome but their own victory.

The enemy proved determined beyond expectation. Spirit matters tremendously; an Orc, fatally pierced in two places, might collapse in despair, or might summon the will to stand once more, amd slice a fatal cut through a human artery before finally falling into the dust.

The Humans already believe that I'm lending the armies my supernatural aid. I'm not; I have other things I need to do. What they face is no more (and not one inch less) - than the adamant dedication of conscious beings who are *absolutely* resolved to spend their deaths in a manner as costly and painful as possible to their foes.

The effect on human morale has been palpable. I'd like to think there's a certain existential horror you face when you believe yourself to be siding with some ultimate good, which always wins, and then you start to *lose*. Whether or not that's true, I can tell you this: every time a human looks into the eyes of an Orc or a Goblin, he doesn't simply see an angry foe. He sees countless generations of unswerving resolve. The army which has emerged from the Dark fights neither like monsters, nor men; it fights like it is trying to break the back of Destiny.

Still, the Human forces *had* been winning. A hundred armories' worth of advanced metallurgy hacked right through more primitive weapons. Years of experience in skirmishes and smaller wars gave advantages in skill, in tactics. And the sight of my Keep, just beyond range of the battlefield, must have been no small incentive.

But then the Orcs realized a thing: every step backwards, either away from the fight, or into death, took them *once again once again not again*--

--back into the dark.

The realization came from no General or Captain; it was not a glorious thing. It came from one tired orc with deep wounds, inflicted in moments when he'd flicked his eyes away from the battlefield and towards that big silly round ball in the heavens, the odd blazing orb which has weighed in on our fate since time immemorial.

He raised his axe, strangely forged, strangely heavy, and said, in a voice nowhere as loud or as resonant as one might expect: "The Sun."

Then the Orc next to him (for neither was that moment engaged with a foe) followed his gaze, looked, *really* looked skyward, and said, a little louder, "The Sun." And suddenly ten thousand Orcs, in almost one voice, said, with mixed awe and wonder, "*The Sun! The Sun!*

**And then there was an army with the honey of Daylight running through their veins. More ecstatic than poison or alcohol: the dream of Returning.**

A few canny human soldiers, near the edge of the battlefield, had planned to survive by hanging back in the heat of battle, and coming forth as the last few darklings fell. (Humans recognize that you need to be alive to write histories the way you want them.) This involved watching their regiment die; but that just adds the tragedy which creates compelling realism, after all. Suddenly those men find themselves at bay.

They're here to fight Evil, and they already "know" that the dark things all have come to steal the sun, to wrench it from the sky. (This does, admittedly seem weird, because even in a world of magic, such an act is beyond the power of all the Gods acting in concert. And if anyone did do such a thing, somehow, the force of gravity would tear the world to pieces and make the whole story meaningless in minutes. Even the uneducated have some idea of this. Nevertheless, there was never a doubt in the minds of Men that justice would prevail, because the only alternative was destruction beyond belief.

And the impossible happens. The Armies of Men fall back.

And they fall back.

And they fall back again.

And that's when, at the very borders of vision, shapes begin flying towards them, from across the horizon.

# Ten Million Arrows

---

**Now look up, ye Goblins, ye Trolls. Here is a moment that will not be forgotten by even the most cynical of written histories: the Elves are coming!**

The Elves have come, in great golden ships, their long hair fluttering behind them carelessly (or at least as carelessly as anything which has been painstakingly styled, over the course of the last century, to specifically look really cool in this moment). The Elves come to save the day—quite literally.

Now there's a word which matches and overruns that cry for the Sun. That word is *Elves*. (Did I mention the ships are gold?)

They're burnished, the ships are. The metal's catching solar rays, making the things of darkness quail. Not from fear, not at first; they just got a dose of sunlight, reflected across the polished metals of the Elven barges.

That's really quite unpleasant. Frankly, the Dark Armies might have been massacred in that moment, had not the humans themselves also looked up, and frankly, they, too, were blinded. Why not? Neither race is immune to the retinal effects of overpowering light. (And that is just how the Elves wanted it. Most everyone blind to everything but the knowledge that they, the Fae, the beloved, honorable Fae, come in the hour of greatest peril.)

In transport both mystical and beyond comprehension arrive the Elves, singing the beautiful songs of their people—

(Not to digress from my own destruction here, but the pedant in me wants to point out that these aren't really the songs of *their* people. It was centuries ago that Elves, who are excellent mathematicians, did an extended study of the theory of musical structure and the tastes of Humans and determined a series of patterns which pleased most the ear. They then outright stole the catchier parts of those weird semi-tonal Orc vocalizations, and added the hammerfall baritone of the Dwarves. In some ways, it's a clever hybrid, and I can admire that, a bit. But it's also the product of those who lacked either knowledge or the caring to create music of their own.)

It's not unlike the way they got much of that gold from the Dwarves they kidnapped. (Wait, I'm sorry, did I say "kidnapped"? I meant "enticed into the shining kingdom through enchanted trips into Fairy portals in the middle of the night which simply *happened* to land them in a place from which the Elves, with the deepest regret, informed them there was no passage back to the mortal realm.")

For the twerps would be needed. (To pound gold onto the ships, that is.) But let it not be said that they went unrewarded. Their bones are now part of some very very pretty tourist attractions in Elfland. And a few of their oldest tunes live on, note-for-note, in the songs of Elf-kind.)

The Elves come singing, stalwart, spotless, as if someone had diligently polished them all before they arrived. They are glory incarnate. The image might be spoiled a bit, perhaps, if more people knew that they were singing, "All right, it's time to give these idiots a show; let's knock in a few heads and bring home some more two-legged pets."

But as I've mentioned, few know the language of the Elves, and those who do love them so much that they never would translate their words with accuracy. If we were graced by the presence of some Human scholar of the Elvish tongue, she'd be waiting for her chance to sleep happily on miles of Orcish corpses and to scribble down some notes about the beautiful serenade. It's not that such scholars are corrupt; it's that if you begin your academic theology already certain of the outcome, none of your research or experience will contradict your beliefs.

It's an important lesson, and one the Elves long-ago perfected: when your mark wants to speak your tongue with joy, let her. She'll find her own interpretation and save you the tedious task of making up your own lies. Give her a translation tome and smile at one or two things she says, she'll be sure she's figured the language like a native. Don't disabuse her. Give her a piece of parchment saying she's an expert, take all her gold as payment (we must make ships!) – and set her loose. If she lives long enough to see you again, she's a success and should come back for the graduate course.

And if an ugly skeptic, like myself, were to speak ill of the Shining Ones, who would believe? Who would take my word over that of—for example--the army currently hovering about our heads, the ones who now hold aloft their longbows in an extremely well-practiced gesture? The Elves and their flying galleons, their gleaming magical transports, they have come at the very moment when all seems lost, when the Orcs, the Goblins, the Trolls, the Hobgoblins, the Kobolds, the things of nightmare seem poised for victory. The Fair Ones have arrived in the instant of humanity's greatest need, born by craft beautiful enough to make you cry, standing there for all the world looking like Justice itself.

Come, it is time to raise a glass in preemptive memory of what is about to happen! An Elvish toast, which is to say Elvish Champagne, which is to say, bubbling fermented blood. Whose blood? None know, and none need to care. The tide has turned; the enemy is suffering terrible losses--

# THE SOUND OF HAMMERS

...And the sun goes out.

No, wait—it's just dimmed.

By an even larger fleet. Inexorable greatships of pure iron—*Elfsbane*—a metal far less malleable than gold, and theoretically immune to most magic, much less the kind of enchantment which would permit something to sail the thermal currents at neckbreaking speeds.

But, given time, research, skill, and obsessively hard work, you can do all manner of seemingly-impossible things.

They come now, flying faster. Vast. So many ships, and so large, that they are like an eclipse, passing between the sun and the Earth, bringing shadow to the ground.

*The ships of the Dwarves.*

For ages, Dwarves have substituted the fire of the Forge for the light of the sun. But that doesn't mean they've ever forgotten what it's like to live in the light. Or forgotten that it's been denied to them.

Where was the Dwarf Army in the alliance of Elves and Men?

Now we know.

Their ships lift higher, with far greater speed than that of the Elves. And why not? Elves are great mages; they live long, they know much, Lore comes easily to them. They are extraordinary with words, and they have chosen to use that to perfect the art of the insult. They've chosen to work hard on internal feuds for the Elfish throne. They have worked hard at appearing to be near unto gods on Earth, harder effort than the average human being would put into raising a family, living a life, and mapping and exploring all of the Hidden Continent. Elvish warriors have senses so keen they can detect a knife without even turning around—because they have spent so long being a hairsbreadth from death at the hands of their brethren.

The Dwarves in my foundries knew of this day. Dwarves in their mines knew it as well. Dwarves, who say little and read much and listen much, who studied history with a stubborn scholarship which lasted generations. Dwarves, considered strange, eccentric misers by humans, considered toys by Elves. An entire species living the in the dark, knowing that their fate was to spend their days immersed in rock, chipping away at it to build ever bigger, more elaborate, more profitable tombs.

How would you choose your fate, if you knew you could either stay shunned in the Underdark, or wait, wait, and then rise up?

And their ships *do* fill the skies, almost literally; you can barely see the firmament through their endless metal hides, and very little light gets past. Over a century of work went into this, and the craftsmanship of thousands of Dwarvish hands. They begin to rain down Hellfire upon the Elves.

(Because you learn a lot of alchemy in the smelting of metals.

And so, too, do you learn patience.)

The Elves fight back valiantly, as would be expected.

But at this moment, there is no Sun in the sky, and the things of the Dark are in their hated—but familiar—element. These are the conditions under which they trained, and they feel at home in the dim light, through which the humans can barely see.

And the Dark Army is again reminded that, if they fail here, then this enveloping shadow is all they will know, all their children will know, all their culture will know, until they forget the light, and know only an unaccountable yearning, unanswerable, but stuck like a dirk in the gut of their descendants, forever.

Demons can only dream of knowing the ferocity with which the darklings now fight. Their curved blades slice through skin and armor alike, such is their fury.

Man will fall.

# DEUS EX MONOKEROS

But wait!

There, glittering like a thing with lots of glitter, effortlessly gliding between the warring aerial brigades, is a creature of extraordinary grace and beauty.

And look!

It has a saddle. It is meant to have a Rider.

Is there anything more beautiful than the sight of the Unicorn, winged, majestic, swooping through a sudden darkness, glowing with its own beauty?

(I may be biased, but I'd say yes: for one thing, it's not like this has done anything to stop the Dwarves from dropping the other ships out of the sky like newly-porous hunks of misbegotten magic, and I'm really enjoying it.) But as the craft of the White Wizard takes fire and nosedives, throwing the Wizard from its deck, the Unicorn aligns itself with his rapidly descending body, and he lands smoothly atop the thing.

(Though "smooth" is a relative turn. I suspect his Wizardly Parts are a tad the worse for wear.)

All is not lost!

Light has saved the day!

*And if you believe that, I've a Unicorn horn to sell you.*

# A Wizard Is Never Early, Because He Doesn't Give A Damn

The Wizard's closest colleagues are not entirely surprised. They waited for the very last, and most dramatic, moment for him to arrive, because he has rather a habit of showing up precisely then. By some "coincidence".

Do *you* know why a Wizard is always on time?

Because if you have a hand in the greatest of disasters, then you might know exactly the instant when hope is at its lowest.

For example: the White Wizard falls, and by either serendipity, or the sheer benevolence of the smiling gods of Good, he's caught. What good luck and/or fate!

Or, a much simpler idea: that winged son of a bitch, the one the Wizard is now riding, was just hanging out in a cloud, watching humanoids die with an inordinate amount of pleasure and waiting around in case something happened to the Wizard's ship.

Long will the bards sing of this moment: Unicorn and Rider unite as one, the Wizard never pausing for an instant, and as the forces of Men who were, a moment ago, terrified, look up, he shouts to them:

*"Take heart! Take heart! It is time to end that which scars the face of our planet!"* He poses with his staff, and bellows. From that wand–at last!–comes a great explosion of radiance, careening outwards in all directions like a beacon gone mad. Dwarven ships (and not a few Elven ships; but who cares?)–blinded, spin away from the field, and the staff pulses again and again, disrupting everything around him. (Call me cynical, but part of me believes this is some of the the the *only* real Magic he knows: symbolic light, no substance, blinding one and all. That being said, it doesn't matter

why he knows this or what it says about his scholarship compared to mine: it's done his work beautifully.)

The Wizard turns to the combat on the ground, but the dark creatures have already started to flee, because they are wretched and cowardly things. (Or so will go the narrative of the humans who survive. And, indeed, a few humans, eager for the kill, turn back to their enemies with the intention of righteous slaughter.)

...But the army which sought the Light is already out of bowshot and retreating rapidly.

The things of the Dark march straight into the mountains, the craggy, difficult landscape where humans could not follow easily, even if the Darklings didn't have a head start. And I can tell you, in this instance, that humans on the battlefield are not precisely inclined to give chase. For they haven't forgotten the slain bodies of their fellows, the savage focus of their foes. More than one soldier has died in the safe-seeming activity of putting a crossbow bolt into the back of a fleeing opponent; it's too easy to forget the prey can turn around. Aside from all of that, with no army in place, the way to my palace is clear. The humans see my military dissolving, and they figure all that remains is me.

The Dwarves regain control of their craft. Perhaps they might fight on. But it's not what they choose. Have they spent too long underground? Has it sapped their wills? Are they merely cowards at heart? For they turn their ships away from the field; they too must know that it's over. The Orcs, the Goblins, the Trolls, the things of Night, they will hide in these mountains a bit. And what will become of them next....

....is another tale altogether. Their ships, perhaps disoriented by the Wizard's sparkly, sparkly power, turn, not in the direction of their faraway mines, but towards the mountains by the battlefield, where it's known that no excavations exist. Perhaps seeing the battle so quickly won, and then so quickly lost again, they plan to dash themselves to death on some remote spire somewhere.

Or they might have somewhere else to be. They might have seen this coming.

It's possible.

The Elves would pursue, but frankly, that would just be slaughter. Which is one of their pleasures in life, but they have their own crisis, one which is endemic to any situation in which those celestial beings, horror of horrors, break a sweat. Calamity: *their make-*

*up is running.* And that is one thing Elves will *not* permit. It is not for other sentient beings to catch more than the briefest glimpse of them without their eyeshadow perfectly in place.

They could do with a bit of mascara, too. They look quite pale, for Elves. They pause to daub their faces with blood.

Interestingly, like their foes, the Elves, too, do not face their ships toward their point of origin, but rather towards the West. It's said that this is the direction of their faraway place of origina, their homeland, whence they might never return. They sing a poignant song of farewell:

"Off we go.

We'd stay, but

Your coffins are tacky."

They're heading to their special place. I'm sure some of them intend to come back. As Rarities, as infrequent emissaries, jaunting to our humble realms from a land they will describe (to their envious listeners) as being so beautiful and perfect, no human could ever set foot there, lest that shining realm be irrevocably harmed by the clumsy touch of a mortal.

I happen to know where they are going. It is something a lot like a desert, with few structures, and just enough water to sustain minimal life. But the Elves don't really care. No one has seen this fabled homeland of theirs, and though it is basically a huge, hostile rocky plain, that doesn't matter, since they permit no visitors. They can name it as they desire; it's some stream of flowing syllables which, they say, means "Elf-home, Place of Peace". That's actually fairly close, by their standards. I'd say it more accurately as "Elf-home, Place Nobody Else Wants". But that's fine, because that is the nature of Elfen ambition. Better to own a dead rock, thinly veiled with sand, and call it a palace, knowing none will know the truth--rather than to stoop to live in an ordinary house and let others see even a moment of imperfection.

The nicest, most carefully furnished parts of Fairyland are the dungeons. Since those are the parts mortals *do* visit.

But I digress.

Now humans have reached my Keep, and the two vast city-sized statues of dragons which are its symbolic guards. Its *mostly*-symbolic guards.

I might, perhaps, have mentioned earlier that I am a Dark Lord. Sometimes I can lie almost as well as a human. About those statues, now...

# What Dragons Breathe Is Not Fire

There remain in this world two Dragons.

They are a mating pair. They will not mate. They do not believe they can repopulate this place, and they are fairly certain that their species can't survive much longer anyway. Dragon eggs don't often make it to term to begin with; the eggs are essentially superheated stone, and they frequently burn up from the inside out. It's the sort of area where humans could perhaps use their endless imaginations to help, if they wanted. But it's more likely that the humans would just set up a restaurant and make extra money on the fact that they're cooking real, authentic Dragon meat over real, authentic Dragon eggs. Because that is the general way things go between Humans and Dragons.

Dragons have two visions of the future. They're not prophetic visions, just extrapolations based on their experience; but that experience has lasted thousands of years, which is why it's helpful to listen. And depressing, since their opinion of the future could be translated pretty much as "Remember that cataclysm which destroyed most life on Earth? Like that, only with more insults."

So assume they raise a clutch of eggs. A few survive. The rigorous process of parenting takes much time and effort, and in this world, there's not much chance of simply settling down and raising a family. Someone, somewhere, will see their wings against the sky and shout, "Dragons!" – and then the horde descends to "eradicate" the wyrms. This pretty much always happens unless the Dragons can find a place that's truly remote, and with Man conquering more mountains and seas, this is less and less likely. Over time, Dragons might lay clutch after clutch of eggs, build a community–and watch humans hunt the members down and slay them, one by one, again and again. Ergo, for obvious reasons, they do not wish to bring children into this world.

This is some of what it means to be a Dragon:

Yes, Dragons are gigantic, and that is part of how we define them, but those are mayfly terms, the understanding of those who seek to cram a lifetime into less than a century and are impressed by parlor tricks, like the ability to bite a warship in half. We think of an intelligence older than ours as simply being, perhaps, a bit smarter or a touch more experienced. That's because we don't like to face how much we change from moment to moment, day to day, how sometimes we shed the skins of our lives every five or ten years and emerge a new product of our experiences.

What happens to a being which thinks through the course of millennia?

Dragons are born with only rudimentary intelligence but retain brain plasticity for a very long time, even as their minds mature. And they are unbelievably long-lived. Perhaps they simply do not die of old age; they just grow in size and knowledge until, and unless, they are killed. So myths suggest, anyway. Very young dragons have little more brain than scorpions or perhaps even little chickens (assuming it ever makes sense to compare barnyard fowl to things which, even at three or four days of age, have claws which slice stone as if it were paper). It's funny to watch the younglings muck about; they're very cute as they seek out food and mock-fight and burn each other a little with rudimentary flame. They *are* rather like little chicks.

(Though we don't recommend actually substituting Dragons for poultry. They are not delicious, and when they friskily open up holes in your body with their sharp hard beaks, you tend to find them less adorable, as the life pours out of you and they playfully splash around in your blood.)

Dragons will not be be domesticated, no matter how impressionable the young ones are, and once they are elders, they likely won't believe a damn thing you say. They have their own Lore; it isn't something humans can really study, because it isn't really a language. This is complicated, not only because they are some of the very few non-bipedal non-humanoid sentients to begin with, but also because, at some point, they decided to store information within themselves, instead of through something external. So Dragons have no writing (though they can, if they choose, write the languages of others). Instead, so far as my studies suggest, they tap into their own Akashic records as a species. That would be impressive enough (so many mages and alchemists of other races have died trying to recapture just a fragment of a past life, much less the library of a whole history!)–except that they don't seem dip into it wholesale. They leave it alone, pulling only certain parts which make up story, song, and dance. And they seem to be able to leave complex trails within the halls of ancestral memory, like sentient bees whose motions convey meaning to others.

No-one has ever cracked Dragon magick.

Once, when I was younger, and less concerned about possible incineration, I had both means and opportunity to ask an old Wyrm why they didn't simply retrieve the whole of their racial memory. I was owed a favor (Dragons do not guard well against theft by lesser beings, much to their sometime-chagrin, and a little human thief might just be better at outthinking a little halfling thief; particularly if the robbed party is a creature so old and powerful that it can't believe anyone would be stupid enough to thieve from its horde.) The Wyrm answered that downloading a thousand lifetimes would grant, not knowledge, but schizophrenia.

Instead, they made their own lizardly decisions of what to hold onto and what to release. Eventually those things were so far removed from what earthbound beings would see as the rudiments of knowledge and language that Draconic speech became impenetrable to others, even when Dragons use the local patois. This is why, when people do converse with them, they're quite cryptic. This is not because Dragons are alien (though they are)–or even because they are hostile; it is because they recognize that human tongues, while marvelous tools, are machines for perceiving reality in very simple terms–"This is what I can feel. This is what I can see. This is what I can taste"–and then making them into absolutes: "...therefore what I see is all there is to see; what I taste is all there is to taste; the way I perceive this thing, here and now, is the truth of the thing."

They grow frustrated trying to explain colors to the colorblind, fragrances to those with no real sense of smell. They feel that beings who speak such limited languages will get trapped within little cage-realities, each one more restrictive than the last. And if there's anything Dragons have learned to hate, in the past ten thousand years, it's a cage.

And thus it is that Dragons want little to do with the affairs of humans. Humans are makers of the most exquisite and intricate prisons. Humans often seem to seek out, not dying (since that's all right; it is possible to die in many worthwhile ways) – but death while alive, a denial of the sentience and agency which gives us meaning; they lock themselves up in reflexes and emotions, until their movements become predictable and you wonder why they don't notice that they go around completely enveloped in their own psychic blinders. It's peculiar how often we act in ways counterproductive the continuation of a species. It must work; we're overrunning the globe, after all. And surely that's a good thing for Man, isn't it? Dominion over all?

But Dragons are unimpressed. Mostly, they're alarmed.

If sheer weight of numbers is the measurement of the value of a species, Man beats other sentients in every way. And thus, Mankind should have the greatest votes, and need not discuss it with other species, right? Men rise; Orcs die; Dragons go extinct; what is there to talk about?

# The Bones of Lizards

Now the great siege weapons are in place, as the humans prepare to defeat my moat and breach my walls. They pause for a moment to take one more look at the imposing Dragon statues, each impossibly tall, which rest before the entrance to my Keep.

**Those aren't statues, fools.**

If human science has been influenced by anything, it might be the discovery of massive bones, serpentine or lizardlike, embedded in rock in obscure places. From this, we might believe that great beasts once walked the Earth.

Or we could believe in Dragons, but then we'd have to face having killed them all.

(Well: *almost* all.)

These two have stood motionless for more than a few human lifetimes, thinking Draconic thoughts. Perhaps they communicate a little, mind to mind. I have never really asked. It is not my business.

They do not guard me out of devotion; they guard me out of practical concern. If you do not think this world is worth bringing your species into, you might consider how you want to die. And if you live particularly long, then you might consider that cessation at some length.

These dragons have decided that they would choose to die—or at least, be deeply likely to do so—on the day that an army of self-proclaimed righteousness comes to break in my door.

It's not exactly they are loyal to me, though I'd like to think that there's a certain kinship among us. It is that I have no desire to go dragon hunting, that I bear them no enmity, that I have no intention of seeking out their hoard. This means much to the lizards. They see humans primarily as apes who invented lances because we distrust anything without opposable thumbs and equally flexible moralities. Humans, in turn, find themselves largely unable to have sane relations with things who bear a form we mostly see in nightmares. The Human army will not sleep well tonight.

They have claws which could make air bleed and breath which is not, as legend would tell you, fire, but rather a stream of heated will, the sort of thing fire would dream of someday becoming, if it had the wit to hope for the unattainable. The Dragons unfold their wings, with a noise like the opening of the gates of the Underworld. And once again, the ground becomes dark; the light of the Sun is neither pervasive enough, nor brave enough, to try to slip past those monstrous scaly things.

They give, in near-unison, a scream which goes straight in through the auditory nervous system, bypassing conscious thought, and makes every mammalian hindbrain scream: "**RUN! RUN NOW!**"

My own blood curdles for a simpler reason, because I know they're calling out their own deaths.

I give the armies of Men credit for attempting to batter down a portal while under attack from Great Wyrms. It's brave. It's not smart, but that's not the point.

Granted, the front gates of my castle do not actually open. They're thrice-reinforced with cold iron and burning spells, and they were never meant for general admittance; this is not a grocery shop, after all. I suppose they might shatter, eventually, if the human army—the remnants of the human army, I should say--are able to bring the necessary force to bear.

The true entrance and exit to my castle is a simple back door, largely unguarded except by the mountains to our back. Had they been wise enough, they might have found their way a bit clearer; but there was no real chance they'd avoid the vast plains of battle in order to trek through the treacherous peaks and boiling geysers to the lee of my edifice. (If they had, many would have perished on the way; you can't really drag a platoon through the crevices of stony highlands and razory crags. You must walk single-file, without your towers and your war-beasts; and you'd be prey for every archer I have. Forcing my armies to meet theirs on solid ground was probably their best bet. That said, the backdoor still might have been wiser than their present course, but we return to the basic idea: while I planned for a few eventualities, I was pretty sure their every impulse would drive them to hurl violence straight at my front door. When you know you've got your dramatic moment to conquer Evil, you want to meet it like something out of the Sagas.

And if you spend a long time pretending the Sagas are true, you set yourself up for forgetting your own lies.

As for that rear entrance—it's not meant to be impenetrable. It's a different kind of test.

There stand my most suicidal, or dedicated, troops. It's just two older humans, still strong, who have done things they wish never to recall. Living here, they don't really care about philosophy or metaphysics. They know they guard this door until eventually, they die from old age and/or overeager young blades. But at least it won't be at the hands of complete idiots; whoever gets to them will have to be at least resourceful enough to get through the labyrinth first.

The White Wizard moved authoritatively through the maze; but after he led them into the third pit trap, the little Chosen One shouldered him out of the way (she's got some biceps growing, that one has) – and took point. She figured out the nature of my rather ironic little geometric riddle, and they're through. As I would have expected, at this point. The company exit the maze and arrive at the hindmost entrance to my home. My old, faithful soldiers give their lives very well in its defense.

I'm not sure if my friends thought they'd end this way. They did know that if anything got through the various traps and portals, it would get through any two soldiers, or, likely, any two hundred. Sure, we originally thought, this was the sort of thing that would happen only if humans decided to waste tens of thousands of lives trying to strike me down. It seemed a poor bargain. But we remembered the basic rule: the only thing stupider than humans in large groups is humans in VERY large groups.

One might wish to change that someday, given the right circumstances. Whatever those might be.

# Diary of the Chosen One: Why Didn't Adventurer's School Teach Us What To Do With All The Corpses?

I haven't written much. What's the point?

Did the Dark Lord think we'd trek through the Wasteland, raise an army, lay waste to her forces (and our own)—just to give us a chance to sneak around to her backdoor?

Apparently so.

Mirthlessly smiling, the White Wizard announces that the Dark Lord is clearly so perverted by evil that it takes pleasure in death and can give no Mercy. I wonder about that. If you're going to be perverted by evil, why waste it on slaughter or running a Realm when you could be drinking a thousand-year wine cellar and having sex with demons?

I'm not going to ask that one.

I suppose I should be happy that our quest nears its end, but it seems like every step brings me closer to hopelessness. The Dark Lord wins; we die. We win; the Dark Lord dies. And then what? The companion, the Man Who Would Behead Anything Smarter Than He Is, becomes King? The White Wizard becomes the Grand Vizier, providing wise and unbiased counsel? I become....what even happens to me, anyway? Princess? Diplomat? Do I have to marry someone? I've never been close enough to royalty to figure out quite what the requirements are, but I suspect "being prematurely bitter and snarky" isn't one of them, which is a pity, because it's what I do best. That, and hunt down Archmages like a faithful hound on a fox-hunt.

I guess, if this all turns out well, I get to go home, to the acclaim of my village. Part of me is a bit cynical, and wonders if they'll even be grateful, now that the danger's over and they don't need me. Part of me, perhaps more cynical yet, wonders if I'll be able to keep from throwing up on them if they are.

I mean, really. Really. You basically could not have been happier to get rid of me. Do you expect me to forget the kicks, the insults, the casual dismissals, the outright disgust you showed me? There's a reason why I spent my time with wandering drunks instead of the hypocrites of my village---and the neighboring villages, for that matter. And the smiles which greeted me when I visited? I truly believe their tiny minds have forgotten (or generously "forgiven") my past. What if I come out of this with a title and nobility and my own castle? I guess there'd be a certain sick satisfaction in watching my former tormentors bow to me as my carriage passed, but who cares? I'm going to face down the Dark Lord within her very home; after I'm done with that, how am I supposed to even pretend I care what some semi-literate plough jockey thinks of me when he's stupid drunk on slightly spoiled homemade beer?

Sometimes, I wonder how the White Wizard lives with himself, but I think the answer is "by never considering the idea that he might be fundamentally wrong". And right now, I think he's in his glory. He loves the power and the attention. I think he believes himself to be a beacon of light. That could be true. But remember:

The right beacon could guide ships safely into harbor.

The wrong one dashes them to death on the rocks.

# IV. If It Appears To Be A Long Time Before The Dawn, That's Because The Sun Has Been Stolen

History is not written in stone. It is written in blood, and countless gallons of it have gone into crossing out and rewriting everything over and over again.

This is what you need to understand about the history of just about anything: It's too glib to say that "History is written by the winners". Yes, as I've often noted, what we see today as historical fact is often a dramatic reinterpretation inspired by one side simply *creaming the heck* out of the other. It's helpful to recognize that Dominion very often takes the form of making it illegal to speak another narrative or to tell another version of the tale, or even sometimes to be who and what you were before you lost. This means that *even* those who have lost will begin to believe the other narrative–because we die without stories, and the winner's tale is the only one left.

And this, in turn, is arguably why the first step of any figure seeking authoritarian rule will be to begin chopping away at speech. If you have the opportunity to fight a great literal war, win a bloody battle, put soldiery through towns and villages; if, in short, by physical force of arms you can set fire to things written in a language you dislike–then you have one means of creating a narrative. But if you do not have that power, or do not want to be seen as welding that noxious force just yet, you begin by the simple process of extirpation. It's like a puzzle: remove a piece and the picture is a little less whole. Remove several pieces and the picture begins to not only look ugly, but to lose meaning. Remove enough pieces and, even though you have left many, perhaps even the majority of the parts of the picture intact, it can no longer can be made out in any meaningful way. And that's when you shout, real loud, that what's there is all there EVER was; that the empty spaces in the puzzle don't matter at all.

Deny the existence of proof. Simply say that everyone knows a certain thing is true and another one false. Say it loudly enough, impale enough heretics who disagree, and it *becomes* true—at least for a while.

And *this* is why the battle for narrative is ultimately more important than almost any other struggle, and why, in the last moments I have, I'll remind you of this piece of Dark Lord ethics:

*You should not fight for the existence of one narrative alone. Not even if doing so makes your life more convenient in the short term.*

It's not about evil or even "wrongness"; it's about *what it will do to your own mind and life* to have no opposition, no disagreement, to not hear any other part of a saga but the ones you like, to consider any other voice to essentially be a disembodied mouth gibbering nonsense. In other words, to see it as something to be hated, something to be pitied, something to be destroyed—but never, for even an instant, something which might have a point.

Is it fair, is it acceptable, to permit something you know as untrue to be spoken? It is; because you're not always right about what is "true". So let more things be said and heard; if Magic teaches us anything, it's that the world can be altered, and actuality is multifaceted. If the cogs of your fiction don't mesh with reality, you'll eventually drive, not creation, but madness.

I could speak on this for a long time, because I think it's really important. And apparently, I'll do so in the face of my own impending end.

My story's unfinished. After all these words--it is unfinished still.

They have what they need to kill me. I really don't want to die.

# Happily Never: On Fairytale Endings

A last testament of sorts. Hear me, Chosen One! This is what is worth dying for: not simply "stories", as some might say, but rather a more slippery, more volatile, more vital thing: the *life* of stories.

Whatever veracity might be, and however it might be attained, you do *not* gain it by some peculiar Darwinian process wherein one particular outlook gains total dominion and all others fade into silence. Perceptions differ, interpretations differ, and the Universe contains multitudes. It's hard to find workable worlds, much less some kind of real understanding, without listening to more than one tale.

Some things are nuanced; most things are simply too complicated to be brought into a binary of yes or no, black or white, live or die. *That doesn't mean there is nothing we can stand on, that nothing is solid or nothing is real. It means that the very fact that we can have reasonable potentialities is based on our ability to deal with partial realities.* Is the door open or closed? Sometimes, you can make a clear distinction: "That door is definitely shut; this door is definitely wide open". Sometimes, you cannot: "The Dark Lord of right now is alive; the Dark Lord of the near future is *probably* dead."

There are some people who won't accept a history that is not written as they wish. They recognize a basic thing: to make the tale they therefore desire, they must destroy opposing histories. **These are the people who become monster-hunters to hide—from themselves, and from everyone else—the fact that they are monsters**.

The simplest, most traditional thing is to make it fell, blasphemous, treacherous, unholy to believe anything but a particular narrative—because that solves so many debates through preempting them completely. "Is such-and-such true? "Well, let me put it this way. If you believe anything else, you are demoniacal and must be cast into the leopard pit. Would you like to ask your question again?"

Whatever happens to me, Chosen, remember:

*Those who seek to destroy every story but their own are an implacable and ultimate enemy. Fight them to death, and beyond.*

# DIARY OF THE CHOSEN ONE: ON JOURNEY'S END

This would be a strange place to hold the end of the tale. If we are not slain, we kill the Enemy, and return to—what, exactly?

A throne, for one of us.

The life of a white-bearded legend, for another.

The eternal suspicion of a small, powerfully-built man, who strangely, did not flee with the rest of his people.

And I—

I am to be recognized in story and song. I am the companion of a Monarch and a Sage. I imagine the food will be good, although I suspect my duties mostly involve wishing the king a long life until such time as he dies from overindulgence in drinking, wenching, and dining, possibly all at the same time.

Soon this all ends, Humanity will be safe, and all the books will speak of a hard-won victory by the White Wizard and his blood-bonded kin, his sworn companions of the heart.

And if I wanted to correct them? If I spent my days at the palace drunk, eccentric, avoided, saying that I am sister to none, that the blood of my body would never mingle with that of the Wizard, that I didn't want any part of what he is or what he'd become?

"Poor lass gone mad from the wars", they'd all say about me.

(But I carried the Dark Lord's heart with me—beating—in a pouch, over my own heart. The two organs often pulse in time; what do I make of that?)

Nevermind.

**Bastards**. Bastards, redoubled in spades; bastards, bastards, **bastards**.

Okay, history. It's you and me. The sooner we get this done, the sooner some bright young scholar can forget my name and leave me out of all this.

# THEY COME

And finally, as certain as misspellings in the book of Fate (I continue to find it frustrating that Fate gets my name wrong)–they breach the defences. They will face a little army of assorted things of the Night before they can get to me. But I have no doubt, strategically, that if they could carve their way through everything else, they will have no real problem with the relatively minor protections of my home, and it will simply result in the demise of the inhabitants thereof. It's not like I've converted my dwelling into some kind of deathtrap; who wants to live in a deathtrap? It would be horribly impractical. "Hey, would you mind washing up your bowls, they're dirty." "I would, but on my way to the kitchen, I fell into a pit trap and had to eat a dozen vipers, and now I'm in a food coma."

Truly, my protections are–were–mostly the fact that it would cost a wastefully insane number of people to bring me down, and honestly, wouldn't it have made more sense to devote those lives to something more useful? Okay, I spread Darkness over my realm and spill some of it out into theirs. What does that even *mean* to them? Do they think I'll spread it everywhere, thus killing all plant life, and from there, all animal life, including myself and my friends? Obviously not; any thinking person would know that would be *insane*. I must have some other plans; but do they ask? No. Why think, when you can rush off in righteous fury?

Frankly, I'd rather the intruders had arrived to an empty castle, but those within were fairly determined to stay. To protect me? Perhaps. I think that's some if it, but mostly, they just seem furious as hell. How weird, eh? These creatures are so surly. It's as if some upstart fanatical sentients had named them "Monsters" and forced them underground forever.

**They die angrily, fiercely, grimly. I am not surprised by it.**

Rule of thumb: anyone who tells you it's not genocide if it's Orcs should be ended with haste.

*The Wizard and companions face my last guardian. It will occupy them a little. It might stop them.* I doubt it, though. There's only one resource I have which might actually kill those pestilential buggers, and it's me. And I think you already know which side I'm betting on.

Still, it gives me a few more moments to reflect; I've muttered the last incantation that makes any sense to me, and anything more would be foolish; some things can't be anticipated, they must simply be met with whatever steel you've got.

*It's strange to be the only one of your kind.* Histories have recorded other Dark Lords; we are not exactly a species, in that we don't seem to be genetically distinct from humans. We just seem to share certain brain patterns and choices which make us reject the normal world, and we seem attracted to this particular archetype. Gods know where it started, or how.

Insofar as I can tell from assorted (questionable) lore, we've all been markedly dissimilar, but in general, Dark Lords are would-be renegades who each raised up a rulership of midnight, exerted some sway on the world, and were all eventually overthrown by sheer weight of numbers and the lack of continuity of line—more specifically, the fact that we do not have successors. We are lone beings. We trust little, and we don't like our species much; reproduction seldom seems to be a primary focus for us. We have brain-children, not actual progeny.

We're limited by that, and by the fact that we seem, in general, to die sooner than we expect. (Isn't that true of most people?) Still, our deaths are generally sudden and violent. I don't know, but I would make a guess that none of my predecessors really had time to think about extension of lineage, because each one was swept away far too soon.

This time might be different. I have communed a little with what I can of the spirits of some of those who came before. I have divined a bit of what I could see of the past. I cannot really know, but I think this is not an ordinary age, and I am, perhaps, not an ordinary Dark Lord—if ever any of us have been "*ordinary*".

This White Wizard isn't exactly typical, either. He is his own breed of madness, though it's true that every time a Dark Lord arises, a prophecy conveniently arises as well. Most of them are fairly brief. The earlier ones are quite unspecific: "Thus shall the Light be forced to destroy the Dark by sticking a sharp thing through some bastard's chest.")

As they evolved, they became flowery to the point of being, if you ask me, fairly revolting. "One day, with the proper stuff and things, there shall arise one whose destiny is writ large and whose eternal glory"--terrible stuff, really.

*This* one? This is perhaps the first prophecy that I have seen which seems to say vastly more about the White Wizard than the Chosen One. It's very impressive. It's written in high Elvish, a language even less understood than normal Elvish, and even more creatively interpreted. The whole ruddy mess is generally translated to mean that when the celestial bodies are correct, there will be born the one whose destiny it is to destroy the Dark Lord. Very standard stuff that, but then it goes on. It says that humankind is precious and lives in a monster-shrouded world, that darkness has always pressed in upon it. and that the greatest threat of all history is *here, present in the flesh*. And that threat *must* be defeated and there can be no concession, no disagreement, no possibility of *anything* but the utter destruction of that being who is constructed of the purest Evil.

I'm *really* curious about that. Because some Dark Lords have threatened the whole Human race with extermination; some Dark Lords have attempted to extend dominion over the whole world. And some...have done things to which no-one can ascribe a motive.

I have never competed for title of the one who does the most damage to mankind. I feel like I probably wouldn't win; that's just not my primary interest. It's always been my simple desire to make things, on behalf of myself and those (should they be found) with whom I have found a kinship. Granted, the ones I've found were unexpected; I'd no idea I'd end up with so many commonalities between myself and the things who have been pushed under the surface of the Earth. An uneasy kinship, sure; we are the sort of kin who might not always get along. It would not shock us if, someday, our relationship leads to violence—or perhaps, to a deeper closeness. It's that kind of family.

I wonder why exactly this prophecy is so Apocalyptic towards me. Do you know what Apocalypse *really* looks like? Like *a flaming thing the size of a continent coming out of the sky. Like all the dead risen up in partial life, with a hunger for moving flesh.* It feels like *plague, a vast one, plague that spreads from every part of every-where to everyone.* It feels like *wrathful Gods plunging the world in-to ceaseless winter.* Apocalypse is when that which has long been under the sea *rises up to claim ownership of the land.* It is when *things from beyond stars we can't even conceptualize* decide that this space should be made into one of their liking, one which could not support on its surface anything which now draws breath.

It doesn't look like *me.*

I would not deny an instant or moment of the darkness which has been my cloak and companion, my drinking buddy, the inky skies which have heard me speak to the Moon so many times--but I am *not* what I am being called. I'm *not* the end of the World. This Prophecy that the world is doomed if I live—it's vague on details, vague on ideas, vague on everything except that Something Needs To Be Done and it needs to be done Regardless Of The Cost. If an army's worth of humans dies just to get to me—well, I guess that's just fine.

It speaks to the human dream of being able to differentiate be-tween the right act and the wrong act as easily as the human eye can differentiate between the lightless back of a cave, and the blinding brilliance of the sun pouring into a clearing.

It doesn't simply appeal to the idea that people want to be Good—and few want to hear, or have others think, that they're Evil. It just ignores the fact that every life is a struggle with potentiality. Every action's a battle for what might be. It's so deeply seductive to believe that you know how to make *this* day into the *right* day every time, into the *best possible day.* It's so much more comfort-ing than the general, existential pain of wondering what a partic-ular hour will bring, what the results of a particular action might be.

But to wonder those things is human. To try to find some algo-rithm which covers all of life is to try, on purpose, to be a machine. Not that I am without my own mechanical aspects; I am a bit of a clockwork thing, always winding myself back up again whenever I begin to drop. But that's not the kind of machine they desire. They want to be the kinds of machines which need never worry about pain or cost. They have the understandable desire to have things go well, have everything taken care of, to drift through life, safe-ly and without ever knowing discomfort. They would never want to be, say, a small human being in a small throne room, in cold fortress surrounded by corpses of friend and foe, waiting for the arrival of one who both can, and believes she should, kill me.

**My last bodyguard was in a space much larger than this room. It was very big. She seemed to have been made primarily of the ability to rend and eat.** It was one of the last of the older, primordial race of Giants, an intractable being who tolerated time in my castle because it was fed well. I, in turn, kept it here because there's no sense in not trying, at least one more time, to end the lives of the invaders before they get to me. I recognized it as probably pointless. But who seeks out the possibility of premature demise when they could attempt to avert it through sensible planning? No one, unless they have a death wish. And I don't wish for anything of the sort. I could say it a thousand times: *My work is not done.* I want to continue to press on. *Death, I defy you. And as no matter when I meet you, there will be no love lost between us.*

And I hear the beast scream, as I knew it would. That's the end of that, and I'm out of time.

They come.

# FALL

---

And here we are, fixed in this moment.

My body is failing. My heart, my literal heart, is in your hands. Your lovely enchanted dagger glows appropriately, waiting to pierce. I can feel the wound already.

*You companions don't see it yet. They think they've won. They think you've won. They're half-right.*

This is not destiny. This was not preordained. This is not wholly my doing, or wholly your doing. This is something we made together, and now it belongs to you.

You drop the dagger. You lift my heart to your mouth.

You bite.

*I cannot speak to the way the thoughts and the knowledge, the memories and the dreams, flow into you. They're in your mind now, and your head will piece them together as you choose. Some will make sense. Some will not. Not everything understood by one is understandable by another, and that is perfectly fine. There's a lot of information in the world, and none of us need grasp it all.*

Everything is possible. Everything is yours. You will have to fight for it every day, re-litigate your existence with the pitiless laws of the Universe on a constant basis.

You are Queen, Empress, God, student, frail organic entity, Maker, Creator, observer, vulnerable mortal thing. I have left you maps, books, keys, tools, treaties, and this diary. I hope they're useful. But I'm not worried about you. I can't predict your future; but I can know your strength, and I suspect you have a lot of world-shaping to do.

To Hell with the White Wizard. To Hell with Prophecy. (And to Hell, quite literally, with me; but Hell is not exactly as the Wizard believes.)

If you don't mind a blessing before I go:

*May you reign supreme but never unchallenged.*

*May you create like a God, but for better, mortal reasons.*

*And, now that the Great Battle is ended, may this be my gift to you--the gift of* **time**. Humans no longer own the Light unchallenged; and *you are* not *alone*. Even now, numberless Orcs recline by a far-off beach, trying to figure out if they can get suntans. But their weapons, and their song, are not far from hand.

Kill your former companions, or turn them to your side; or set them loose to oppose you. Whatever you do, you've already changed history. Let's see the bastards rewrite *this*.

(But they'll try. You'll just have to write it better.)

I am the first Dark Lord in a thousand years. You are the second, and your path has been unlike that of any who proceeded you; unlike mine, even. Just your own. Only you decide what you will create, what you will seek, and what decisions you will make when the White Wizard finally realizes what happened. You know this, but allow me the dying creature's small pleasure of stating the obvious: *Your legacy is in your bloodied hands. Go use them.*

You, in rising, embrace the Night; and I, in falling, do the same.

I hear the hungry Moon. She calls. I come home.

END.

CPSIA information can be obtained
at www.ICGtesting.com
Printed in the USA
BVHW081753090919
557952BV00014B/1796/P